Gargoylz

Triple Trouble!

Gargoylz: grotesque stone creatures found on old buildings, spouting rainwater from the guttering. Sometimes seen causing mischief and mayhem before scampering away over rooftops.

www.kidsatrandomhouse.co.uk

Read all the Gargoylz adventures!

Coming soon!

Gargoylz

Triple Trouble!

Burchett & Vogler
illustrated by Leighton Noyes
RED FOX

GARGOYLZ TRIPLE TROUBLE!
A RED FOX BOOK 978 1 849 41170 7

First published in Great Britain by Red Fox,
an imprint of Random House Children's Books
A Random House Group Company

This edition published 2010

1 3 5 7 9 10 8 6 4 2

Series created and developed by Amber Caravéo
Copyright © Random House Children's Books, 2009
The Random House Group Limited supports the Forest Stewardship Council
(FSC), the leading international forest certification organization. All our titles
that are printed on Greenpeace-approved FSC-certified paper carry the FSC
logo. Our paper procurement policy can be found at
www.rbooks.co.uk/environment

Set in Bembo MT Schoolbook

Red Fox Books are published by Random House Children's Books,
61–63 Uxbridge Road, London W5 5SA

www.**kids**at**randomhouse**.co.uk
www.**rbooks**.co.uk

Addresses for companies within The Random House Group Limited can be
found at: www.randomhouse.co.uk/offices.htm

THE RANDOM HOUSE GROUP Limited Reg. No. 954009

A CIP catalogue record for this book is available from the British Library.

Printed and bound in Great Britain by CPI Bookmarque, Croydon, CR0 4TD

Hello, I'm the Web Gargoyle.
Look out for me – I'll be hiding in one
of the pictures in the book.
When you spot me, be sure to make a
note of the secret codeword I'm holding.
The codeword unlocks a secret level
of the amazing Gargoylz game
on our fabulous website at
www.gargoylz.co.uk

Oldacre Primary School

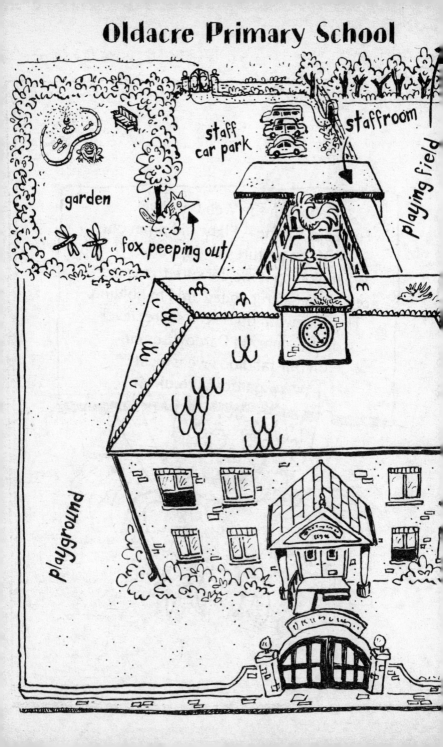

St Mark's Church

playground

School Report - Max Black

Days absent: 0

Days late: 0

Max is a bright boy. If he spent as much time on his school work as he does on annoying Lucinda Tellingly he would get much better marks. I am pleased to see that he enjoys exercise – although I do not count running down corridors making racing car noises. Also I would be glad if he did not shout "Awesome" quite so loudly every time we have football practice.

Class teacher - Miss Deirdre Bleet

The only good thing I can say about Max Black is that he is always early for school. However, he is the last one into the classroom. He spends far too much time playing tricks with Ben Neal. Mrs Pumpkin is still off sick after discovering an earwig farm in her handbag. Max ignores all school rules. He has recently developed a curious interest in drainpipes and has been seen talking to the wall. This behaviour is outrageous and must stop.

Head teacher - Hagatha Hogsbottom (Mrs)

School Report - Ben Neal

Days absent: 0

Days late: 0

Ben has many abilities which he does not always use. He works very hard at dreaming up tricks to play, which gives him very little time to concentrate on his learning. He enjoys football and skateboarding - indeed, he and his board can frequently be found upside down in a flowerbed.

Class teacher - Miss Deirdre Bleet

Ben Neal is a strange boy. He is often to be found grinning at gutters.

He constantly breaks school rule number 742: boys must not break school rules.

Ben thinks he can get away with anything by flashing his blue eyes and looking innocent. I am not fooled. Indeed I am still waiting for him and Max Black to write a note of apology to Mr Bucket the caretaker. Gluing his wellington boots to the staffroom ceiling was outrageous!

Head teacher - Hagatha Hogsbottom (Mrs)

Contents

Book One:
Gargoylz on the Loose!

1. Toby Turns Up

Max Black zoomed out of his front door.
He was playing his usual game on the
way to school. He was a nine-year-old
secret agent, speeding along in his super-
powered spy plane.

"MAX!"

He skidded to a halt,
trainers smoking. His
mum was standing in the
front garden.

"You've forgotten your
school bag again!" she called,
holding it out.

1

Max ran back and snatched it up.

"Did you brush your hair this morning?" demanded his mother.

"Yes, Mum." Of course he hadn't. He'd lost his brush down the toilet months ago. His dark brown hair stuck up all over the place and that was how he liked it.

Max set off along the pavement again. There was a boy ahead of him dribbling a football. Max activated his spy radar to check him out: blond hair, blue eyes, big grin, nine and a quarter years old.

He knew what that meant. It was Ben Neal, codename: Best Friend.

Max sneaked up behind him. "Agent Black ready for action," he hissed in Ben's ear.

Ben grinned and passed the ball to Max's feet. "New spy mission," he yelled, running ahead. "Get football to school at top speed."

They were soon at the gates. Max looked up at Oldacre Primary School, sandwiched between the ancient stone church and the post office.

"Another day of torture," he groaned.

"Bell's not rung yet," said Ben. "Let's practise some nifty football skills."

"You're on," said Max as they ran through the playground. His spy radar homed in on someone: pale, skinny, face like a weasel. Max knew what that meant. It was Enemy Agent Lucinda Tellingly, codename: Bossy Boots. "Bet you can't lob the ball right over Lucinda's head."

SPY FILE:

codename: Bossy Boots

"That'll be hard," said Ben. "She's got the biggest head in the world!"

Lucinda was standing near the netball hoop. Ben placed the ball carefully on the ground and took three steps back.

"Watch," he said. "Straight over her head and through the hoop."

Wham! Up went the ball. Down it came – **thump!** – right on top of Lucinda's ponytail. It bounced off sideways and landed on the low flat roof over the staffroom.

"Now look what you've done, Lucinda," moaned Ben, peering up at the ball. "It's stuck."

"Good!" snapped Lucinda. "I hope you never get it back." Lucinda didn't like Max and Ben – the boys had no idea why.

Just then, the bell rang for the beginning of school and Lucinda stomped off, tidying her ponytail.

"How am I going to get my ball down?" sighed Ben, ignoring the bell.

"We could try a fishing rod with glue on the end," suggested Max.

Ben's eyes lit up. "Brilliant plan, Agent Black." Then he frowned. "There's just one tiny problem – we don't have a fishing rod."

"Then we'll have to get onto the roof," said Max. "And I know how. We'll climb

up on that skip in the teachers' car park."

The skip was full of old furniture. Using a bookcase as a ladder, the boys were soon up on the staffroom roof.

Suddenly there was a skittering, scrabbling noise behind them. They whirled round.

Their eyes nearly popped out of their heads. A very peculiar creature was bounding towards them. It was the size of a puppy and it scampered along on all four paws. It had a monkey face with long pointy ears and golden eyes that glinted in the sunshine. Its skin looked exactly like the stone on the church next door.

Leafy wings sprouted from its back and its dragon-like tail wagged merrily.

The creature skidded to a halt, squatted on its hind legs and gave Max and Ben a huge grin.

"I think it's a gargoyle!" whispered Max.

"Do you mean one of those stone things on the church?" asked Ben.

"Yes," said Max. "They hang under the gutters and spout rainwater."

"But it can't be a gargoyle," Ben objected. "Gargoyles are just statues. They're not alive."

"This one is," said Max, staring.

"Greetingz," said the gargoyle merrily. His voice was a mixture between a growl and a purr – like a sort of dog-cat. "I'm Tobias the Third. You can call me Toby. I live on the church porch." He put his head on one side and peered at them. "Spluttering gutterz!" he chortled. "Are you school gargoylz? You're the ugliest ones I've ever seen."

"We're not gargoyles," Max told him.

Toby's impish face creased up in a frown. "Of course you're gargoylz!" he said. "You were climbing on the roof and making mischief. Only gargoylz do that." He gave Max's arm a pinch. "Your stone is a bit flabby though."

"We're not made of stone," Ben explained.

"We're boys. I'm Ben and this is Max."

Toby looked horrified. "You mean you're humanz? But humanz aren't supposed to know that gargoylz are alive!

What am I going to do?" He began to wail and bite his claws.

"We won't tell anyone about you," Max shouted above the noise. "We promise, don't we, Ben?"

"I promise never to tell a soul that gargoylz are alive," Ben said solemnly. He picked up his football. "Cross my heart and may I never play with this again if I do."

Toby perked up immediately. "Glad we got that sorted out," he purred.

A booming voice suddenly rose from below. "What are you boys doing?"

Toby looked startled. "Freeze!" he whispered. He squatted on his haunches, put on a frozen, wide-mouthed snarl and kept absolutely still. Now he looked just like the gargoyles on the church.

Max peered cautiously over the guttering. He activated his spy radar: grey hair, beaky nose, steam coming out of ears. He knew what that meant.

It was Enemy Agent
Mrs Hogsbottom,
commonly known
as Mrs Hogsbum,
codename: Evil
Head Teacher.

"Outrageous!" she
screeched at them.
"Get down at once!"

Max and Ben got down.

"I might have known it would be you
two," the head teacher said, studying
them with her laser vision. "If there's any
trouble, Max Black and Ben Neal are
always behind it! I have not forgotten your
spaghetti forest in the teachers' toilet last
week. Poor Mr Widget still turns pale at
the mention of pasta."

"But we were just trying to brighten
the place up a bit—" Ben protested.

"Silence!" snapped Mrs Hogsbottom.
"The school bell has rung and where do I

find you? Running about on the roof."

"We weren't running, miss," Max tried to explain. "We—"

"No arguing!" ordered Mrs Hogsbottom fiercely. "School rule number fifty-six: children must not argue."

Ben put on his special wide-eyed innocent face. It always worked on the dinner ladies, who gave him extra sausages. It never worked on Mrs Hogsbum. Her bony fingers shot out and snatched the football from him.

"But—" began Max.

"Get to your classroom at once!" snapped the head teacher.

"When can I have my—?" began Ben.

"You can have your football back at the end of the week," snarled Mrs Hogsbum as she stormed off, "and not before!"

"How ungrateful!" fumed Max. "Especially when we saved the caretaker all the trouble of having to fetch it for us." He looked up at the roof. "Toby? Are you still there?"

There was a scrabbling sound and then the gargoyle's chirpy little face appeared over the edge of the gutter. "Glad that ugly monster's gone," he said.

"She's worse than a monster," Max told him. "Monsters run away when they see *her*."

"And now she's got my football," grumbled Ben. "I bet that's the last I'll see of it."

"She might burst it with her horrible

sharp nose," said Max.
"Or flatten it under
a pile of maths books,"

said Ben.
"Or cut
it into tiny
pieces and
boil it up in her
cauldron," Max added.
"I know what will
cheer you up," grinned
Toby. "I'll show you
how I can fly. It's my
special power."
"Awesome!" said Ben,
football forgotten.
But before Toby
could move, Mrs
Hogsbottom's head

popped out of the staffroom window like a fearsome jack-in-the-box. "Off to class!" she bellowed. "IMMEDIATELY!"

The boys scampered for the door. Max looked back to wave at Toby, but the gargoyle had gone.

"Did you see Toby's wings?" whispered Max as he and Ben bent over their class maths test. "I can't wait to see him fly."

"And he talked about making mischief," said Ben. "He's our sort of gargoyle!"

"I've just had a brilliant idea," declared Max. "We must get to the girls' loo – now."

Ben looked horrified. "You call that a brilliant idea? I wouldn't be seen dead in that stinky place. It's all clean and flowery!"

"True," Max agreed. "But if you look out of one of the windows up there, you can see the staffroom roof. We might spot Toby again."

"Good thinking, Agent Black," said Ben.

"That *is* a brilliant idea. There's just one problem – we need to come up with a way to get out of here."

"Max and Ben!" snapped a voice behind them.

Max's spy radar told him what that meant: short and dumpy, limp brown hair, silly half-moon glasses. It was Enemy Agent Miss Bleet, codename: Wimpy Teacher.

"Wasting time chatting, are we?" sighed Miss Bleet. She always sounded tired when she spoke to Max and Ben. Max thought she should go to bed earlier. "Ben, go and sit with Poppy," she went on. "Max, stay where you are. Then you might both do some work."

"See you in the girls' loos," Max hissed as Ben

SPY FILE:

codename:
WIMPY
Teacher

pushed his
chair back noisily.
Max chewed his
pencil. He was just
wondering how to escape
when a paper aeroplane
sailed past Miss Bleet, who nearly fell into
the wastepaper bin in fright. The missile
banked and turned and hit Max on the
ear. He picked it up. It was Ben's maths
test – beautifully folded.

"Ben Neal!" quavered their teacher.
"Go and stand outside in the corridor."

Max was impressed. Who'd have
thought that a boring test
could be so useful? It had
got Ben out of class. Now
it was his turn to escape.
He stuck up his hand.

"Can I go to the toilet
please, miss?"

"You'll have to wait till playtime," Miss Bleet said, looking impatient.

Right, thought Max, *time for Secret Plan: Bursting.* He crossed his legs and bounced up and down on his seat. "Oooh, miss!" he groaned.

But for once Miss Bleet wasn't budging.

Time for Secret Plan: Explosion, Max thought. He held his breath and crossed his eyes.

"He's going to wet himself!" squealed Lucinda.

Max let out a terrible moaning sound. Lucinda shrieked, and Tiffany and Shannon moved their chairs away. Everyone in the class craned their necks to watch.

"OK, you can go," said Miss Bleet hurriedly. "But come straight back."

Max was out of the classroom before she could say homework. He sprinted down the empty corridor, leaped up the

stairs two at a time and burst into the
girls' toilets.

Ben's head peeped out of one of the
cubicles. He beckoned to Max. "I've found
the right window."

Max squeezed in and pushed the door
shut behind him. There was a small open
window above the toilet.

Ben climbed on the seat. "Get up here,"
he said. "It's a great view. But the seat's a
bit dodgy."

Max scrambled up next to him and they
clung to the window ledge, peering out.

"ROOAARR!"

A terrifying, snarling face appeared at the window right in front of them.

"Yow!" cried Max, jumping backwards and knocking into Ben.

CRACK!

The toilet seat broke off its hinges and the two boys tumbled to the floor.

Max sat up. Ben was sitting next to him, the toilet seat round his neck. Max could hear chortling. He looked up at the window to see Toby sticking

his tongue out at them, his golden eyes shining with mischief.

Suddenly the cubicle door burst open. Toby ducked out of sight.

"Max Black and Ben Neal!" exclaimed Miss Bleet. "What are you doing in the girls' lavatories? And *why* are you wearing a toilet seat, Ben?"

"I'm not wearing it, miss," began Ben dizzily. "I was just—"

"I don't want to hear any excuses," sighed Miss Bleet. "You can both spend playtime *and* lunch time tidying the stock cupboard."

"Boring," grumbled Max as they trailed back to class. "Bet she won't let us run beetle races or stick crayons up our noses like we did last time."

"And we won't be able to see Toby again till after school!" added Ben miserably.

For the rest of the day Max and Ben did everything they could to get out of the classroom, but nothing worked – not even when Max told Miss Bleet he'd been bitten by a super-poisonous spider and needed to go to the nurse.

When the bell went, they were first through the door.

"Can you see Toby?" yelled Max as they ran into the playground.

"Not a claw in sight," answered Ben.

Max stopped. A horrible thought had hit him. "Do you think he's gone for good?"

Ben shook his head. "Can't have. He's probably back home on the church."

"Good thinking, Agent Neal," said Max. "Let's search there."

They ran into the churchyard.

"There he is!" shouted Ben, pointing up at the porch. "But he's not moving."

The little monkey-like stone creature was hanging just under the guttering, his mouth in a wide, fixed snarl.

"Hey, Toby," called Max. "Remember us?"

The stone eyes didn't blink. They just stared blankly over the churchyard.

"What's wrong with him?" asked Ben. A look of horror came over his face. "We didn't imagine it, did we?"

"No," Max hissed, pointing. "That's the answer. He's seen Mrs Hogsbum coming."

Their head teacher was steaming down the path towards them.

"What are you doing here?" she demanded. "Have you lost a football on the church roof? School rule number one hundred and thirty-three: boys must not lose footballs on the church roof."

The boys shook their heads.

"HURUMPH!" Mrs Hogsbottom glared suspiciously at the guttering.

There was a very rude noise and a **whoosh**, and suddenly a flood of dirty rainwater spewed from Toby's open mouth straight into the head teacher's face.

Max and Ben burst out laughing. Mrs Hogsbum's grey hair was plastered to her head like a swimming cap.

A tangle of leaves and old pine cones
was stuck over one ear and her mascara
had run. She looked like a
demented zebra.

"Outrageous!" she spluttered as she squelched back to school. "Go home this instant!"

Toby launched himself off the gutter and zoomed around the boys' heads, doing victory loop-the-loops.

"Spluttering gutterz!" he yelled as he went. "That's the best trick I've done since I dropped a slug on the vicar's head in the middle of a wedding."

"It was awesome," laughed Max. "And you can really fly! That's awesome too!"

"*Totally* awesome!" agreed Ben, watching Toby swooping up and down in glee.

Toby waved merrily. "Got to go. See you!" And, with that, he flew over the church tower and out of sight.

"I never thought I'd say this," said Ben, "but I'm really looking forward to school tomorrow."

"Me too." Max grinned. "We're going to have the best fun ever now that Toby's our friend!"

2. The Big Stink

Max and Ben zoomed along the road on Ben's skateboard. Today they were secret agents working undercover as racing drivers. They swerved in through the school gates, hit a dustbin and fell off into a bush.

"Record speed in the World Championships!" exclaimed Max, brushing twigs out of his hair.

31

"Cool spin at the last bend," agreed Ben as he inspected his skateboard for damage.

Max glanced around the playground and dropped his voice like a good spy. "Today's mission – find Toby!" He looked eagerly over the school wall at the church porch, where their new gargoyle friend lived. "I wonder what tricks he'll play today."

"Out of my way!" came a harsh voice.

Max activated his spy radar: shaved head, big fists, evil scowl. He knew what that meant. It was Enemy Agent Barry Price, also known as The Basher, codename: School Bully.

Barry stomped around with a nasty smirk on his face. Some reception kids were standing in a line, taking it in turns

to play hopscotch – at least they were until
The Basher bashed into them. They fell
down like skittles.

"Hide!" whispered Max. "We don't
want to be next."

The boys ducked down behind the
dustbins.

There was an evil glint in The Basher's
eye as he marched towards some girls who

were skipping, but before he could reach them, he leaped into the air with a shriek, clutching his bottom. An acorn fell to the ground and rolled away.

Barry spotted the acorn and snatched it up. "Who threw that?" he snarled.

Max and Ben had to stifle their giggles as another acorn hit The Basher on the nose. There was a wheezy sniggering sound above them. Max's spy radar snapped into action: monkey face, big pointy ears, wicked grin. He knew what that meant. It was Toby, their gargoyle friend. He was peering down from the church roof – and he had a catapult in his paw.

"Hi, Toby!" yelled Max. They ran over

to the wall by the churchyard.

"Greetingz," the gargoyle called in his growly purr. "Can't stop. Bit busy."

Whizz! Ping! Whoosh! He fired off a barrage of acorns. The Basher leaped like a jumping bean all over the playground as the mini missiles bounced off him. At last he fled round the corner.

"So you were the one firing at The Basher!" said Ben, impressed. "Serves that bully right."

"We got rid of him!" said a timid voice

from the roof. The boys could just see
a pair of rabbitty ears sticking up
behind Toby.

"Hey, Toby," Max called. "Who's that?"

"This is Barnabas," announced Toby.
"He lives on the church tower. He's my
friend." He beckoned with a claw. "Come
and say hello, Barney."

The new gargoyle slowly waddled to
the edge of the roof. He had a face like
a soppy dog, with round, solemn eyes. All

down his back was a ridge of spikes that reminded Max of a stegosaurus.

Barney took one look at Max and Ben and began to shake like a jelly. "Humanz!" he whimpered. "But humanz aren't supposed to know that gargoylz are alive. What are we going to do?" He froze, his eyes glazed and a terrible pong filled the air.

"**PHWOAAHH!**" gasped Max, holding his nose. "What's that?"

"Smells like the stinkiest stink bomb *ever*!" spluttered Ben, backing away.

"Smellz is Barney's special power," said Toby. "Just like mine's flying."

"And drenching head teachers!" added Max.

"All gargoylz can empty gutterz from their mouths," said Toby. "That's easy – but when Barney does a bottom burp, everybody runs." He cupped his paw to his mouth so that only the boys could hear. "Trouble is, sometimes he gets nervous and makes the smell by accident."

"It's an awesome power," said Max. "I wish I could do it. Don't be scared of us, Barney. We won't tell anyone about you."

Barney twitched an ear and slowly came back to life.

"This is Max and Ben," explained Toby. "They're full of tricks, just like us gargoylz."

"Pleased to meet you," whispered Barney. He wrinkled his nose and sniffed the air like a dog. "What's that delightful smell?"

"Doesn't he know it stinks?" gasped Ben in amazement.

But the gargoylz weren't listening.

"I can smell it too," said Toby, his golden eyes shining. "It's *wonderful*!"

"It's coming from that funny-looking human with her tail on her head," said Barney. "You didn't tell me humanz could make smellz like that."

Puzzled, Ben and Max sniffed. As Barney's pong faded away, they got a wonderful whiff of warm, freshly baked cookie.

Max gazed longingly in the direction of the smell. Someone was clutching a cake tin. His spy radar went mad: pale, skinny, face like a weasel. Max knew what that meant. It was Enemy Agent Lucinda Tellingly.

"Lucinda's been baking," gasped Max.

"Happy birthday, Poppy," they heard her say in her shrill voice. "I made these specially. The biggest one's for you."

"What a creep," muttered Max.

"Those cookies look awesome though," said Ben. "I want one."

Lucinda was passing the tin around to her friends. "Help yourselves," she said smugly.

Max winked at Ben and grinned. "Don't mind if I do!" He leaped onto the skateboard and sped across towards the girls. As he passed by, he snatched a cookie from the tin.

"I'll get you for that, Max Black," Lucinda yelled after him. "You wait!"

"I was just helping myself like you said," Max called back, expertly flipping the skateboard to a stop by the wall.

The cookie was still warm and bursting with gooey chocolate chips. Max saw three pairs of eyes on him. He sighed and broke it into four pieces.

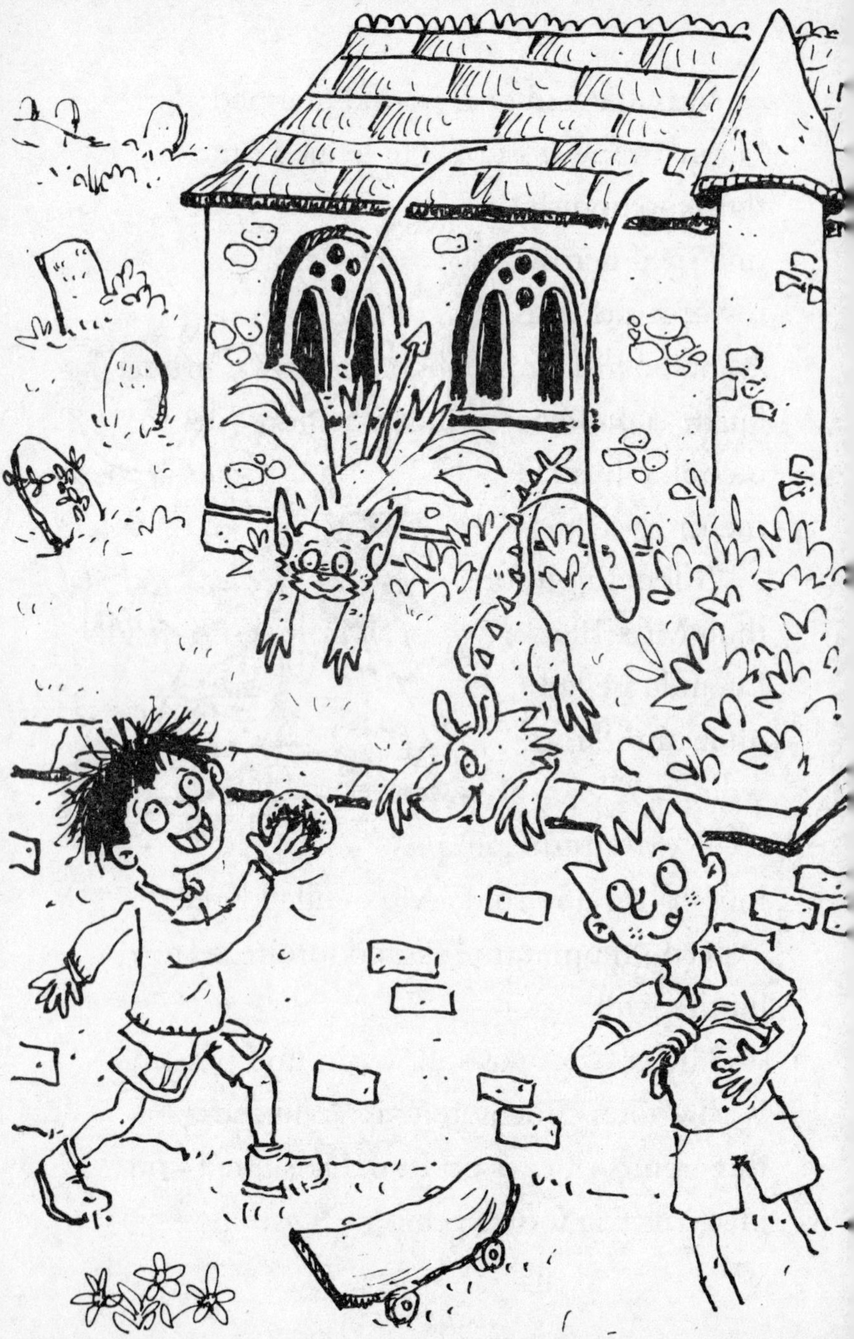

Toby and Barney jumped down from the church roof onto the wall. They grabbed a piece each.

"What do we do with them?" asked Toby.

"I'll show you." Ben laughed and gobbled his chunk of cookie down in one gulp. "I don't care what Lucinda does to us after this," he sighed, rubbing his tummy. "It was worth it."

Toby and Barney looked at each other, then stuffed their pieces of cookie in their mouths like Ben. Huge smiles spread across their stone faces.

"Nice," said Toby.

"Nice?" gasped Barney, chocolate smeared all over his doggy nose. "It's *delicious*!"

Just then the bell rang. Max heard heavy footsteps behind him. He turned. It was Mrs Hogsbum.

Toby and Barney froze right there on the wall, faces covered in chocolate.

As usual Mrs Hogsbottom made a

beeline for the boys.
"School rule number
two hundred and
twenty-seven,"
she began.
"Boys must
not stand next
to walls and
look innocent
when—" She
stopped and
gawped at the unexpected stone figures on
the wall.

"Are you all right, miss?" asked Max.

"Did you put those . . . things . . . there?"
demanded Mrs Hogsbottom, turning to
stare at the two boys.

As she turned, Toby and Barney
disappeared behind the wall.

Ben opened his eyes wide and
attempted to look innocent. "What things,
miss?" he asked sweetly.

Mrs Hogsbottom looked back at the now-empty wall. Her eyes bulged. "Outrageous!" she spluttered.

"I think you need to sit down, miss," said Max kindly. "You're not getting any younger. We'll take you inside."

"See you," Max heard faintly as he and Ben led their gibbering head teacher away.

★ ★ ★

Toby and Barney didn't reappear at playtime or lunch time.

"There's not even a whiff of a pong," moaned Max as they went in for afternoon lessons.

"It's been such a boring morning," complained Ben. "Miss Bleet even stopped us doing our woodlouse Olympics up and down the table."

"She wouldn't listen when I said they needed their exercise," added Max sadly.

"Shame Lucinda didn't try and get revenge for the cookie-theft," said Ben. "At least that might have been interesting."

"I expect she's chickened out," answered Max.

"Hey, I've just remembered," said Ben, cheering up suddenly. "We've got football now."

Max brightened too and the boys sped into the cloakroom to change, leaving their clothes in the usual messy pile on the floor.

"Last one on the field is a banana!" yelled Max as they burst into the corridor and dodged one of the girls.

"Out of the way, Lucinda!"

"That was a great match," said Max, admiring the mud splodges on his arms. "We only lost by one goal." He and Ben bounded into the boys' cloakroom.

"What's that smell?" gasped Ben, staggering backwards. "It's . . ."

"Sweet . . ." said Max.

"Flowery . . ." added Ben.

"Hideous!" shuddered Max, flapping his hand in front of his nose.

Duncan laughed. "And it's coming from *your clothes*," he told them.

Max and Ben picked up their uniforms. All the boys were laughing now.

"They stink!" wailed Ben. "Someone's put perfume all over them."

"Yeeuurgh!" said Max, looking furious. "I bet I know who did it . . ."

"Lucinda Tellingly!" the boys cried together.

"She's got her revenge – we can't wear our uniforms like this," said Ben in disgust.

"We could keep our football kit on instead," suggested Max.

"Miss Bleet would have a fit if we did that!" Ben said.

Then he grinned. "It might be fun."

"But then she'd ban us from football for a month," Max pointed out. He held his nose and started pulling on his uniform. Ben groaned and did the same.

They made their way back to the classroom, leaving a trail of flowery pong behind them. As they came in, the whole class turned to see what the smell was.

A wave of laughter rippled round the room and Max noticed that Lucinda had a smug smile on her face.

"This is war!" he muttered to her. He slid into his seat and hunched down, trying to be invisible.

"Quiet now, please," called Miss Bleet. She beamed at the class. "I hope you've all remembered to study your lines."

There were eager nods all round.

"Oh, no," whispered Ben. "It's drama and I didn't learn my words for that stupid play she wrote about pixies."

"Me neither," said Max. "Miss Bleet's going to be furious . . . No, wait a minute, I've just had a fantastic idea! I know how to get us out of trouble *and* have our revenge on Lucinda at the same time!" He started rummaging in his rucksack. "Thought so," he said after a moment. "I've still got Old Pongo!" He showed Ben a small round ball.

"A stink bomb!" Ben was delighted. "Good plan. She stank *us* out, so

51

we'll do the same to her."

"Watch this." Max rolled the ball expertly under Lucinda's chair. "She's bound to step on it, and Miss Bleet won't bother about *us* when she gets a whiff of Old Pongo."

Soon it was Lucinda's turn to say her lines. She was Chief Pixie.

She pushed her chair back to stand up. The stink bomb was right under her foot. Any minute now . . .

"What's that?" asked their teacher suddenly. Just as Lucinda's foot came down, Miss Bleet fished the ball out from under it. She frowned at it suspiciously, then plonked it on her table. Lucinda flung out a dramatic arm and began.

"We've had it," Max groaned to Ben as the Chief Pixie squeaked through her lines.

"Things can't get any worse. We smell like a flower shop *and* we're going to get into mega trouble for not knowing our lines."

But Ben wasn't listening. He was pointing to Lucinda's bag, which lay at her feet. Max looked down. A cheeky monkey face was poking out of it.

"Toby!" Max gasped under his breath.
Their small friend waved merrily at them.

"And Barney!" whispered Ben as the
little gargoyle popped up next to Toby.

"Barney with the special power of a
stink bomb!" Max's eyes lit up. "We're not
going to get into trouble after all – as long
as I can get Barney to understand that we
need one of his really strong pongs."

Max held his nose and pulled a
revolting face at Barney, as if he could

smell something awful, but shy Barney
went bright red and covered his eyes.
Max decided to see if he could get Toby
to understand instead. Then *he* could
explain to Barney. He pulled a face at Toby.

Toby pulled a face back.

"It's not a game," Max muttered to
himself. "We need a stinker." Lucinda had
almost finished and it was his turn next!

He held his nose, flapped his hand
in the air in desperation and pointed at

Barney. A grin slowly spread over Toby's face. He grabbed his friend by one ear and whispered into it. After a moment Barney nodded enthusiastically, then his eyes glazed and a few seconds later an appalling smell rose from underneath Lucinda's chair. Toby and Barney ducked speedily out of sight, sniggering.

The class leaped to their feet, coughing and spluttering. Duncan put his PE bag over his head.

"Lucinda . . ." croaked Miss Bleet, clamping a hankie over her face as her eyes started to water.

"It wasn't me, miss!" said Lucinda indignantly. She glared at Max and Ben. "I bet it was—"

But Miss Bleet wasn't listening.

"Everybody out!" she ordered, shooing the class towards the door. "Make for the playground."

"It's like fire drill," said Max in delight.

"Stink drill!" Ben laughed.

There was a rush for the door. Lucinda was at the front of the queue.

Soon everyone had gone.

Toby and Barney popped out of their hiding place and perched on Miss Bleet's table. Holding their noses, the boys dashed over to them.

"That was great!" Ben told the gargoylz. Toby grinned. "Barney's best trick since  he stank out the vicar's Christmas party," he said.

Barney grinned too.

"But what were you doing in Lucinda's bag anyway?" asked Max.

Toby and Barney looked a bit sheepish.

"We were on a cookie hunt," explained Toby. "That one this morning was so scrumptious."

"But we couldn't find any," put in Barney, looking disappointed.

"You deserve all the cookies you can get your paws on!" exclaimed Max, finding it was safe to stop holding his nose.

"It's thanks to you we're not in trouble," added Ben. "And everyone thinks Lucinda made the stink! We win all round."

Barney bounced up and down on the table in excitement.

"No, Barney!" yelled Toby.

But it was too late. Another dreadful stench was filling the air.

"I forgot to say," said Toby, scooting off to the window. "Barney makes stinks when he's excited as well."

"Uh-oh!" yelled Max and Ben. "Wait for us!"

3. Spider Surprise

DER-RING!

"Answer the door, please," yelled Max's mum from upstairs.

Secret Agent Max Black threw open the front door and aimed his super spy-zapper at the intruder. Ben stood there, dangling a huge hairy spider in front of Max's nose.

"Awesome, Agent Neal!" breathed Max.

"His name's Sidney," Ben told him. "He looks real, doesn't he? I put him on my mum's cornflakes at breakfast. I thought she'd never come down from the ceiling. Then Arabella ruined it by telling her it was a toy. Sisters!"

Max caught sight of something at the top of the stairs. He activated his spy radar: small, shriekingly loud and extremely annoying. He knew what that meant. It was Enemy Agent Jessica Black, codename: Disgusting Little

Codename:
Disgusting
Little Sister

SPY FILE:

Sister. She was in the middle of brushing her teeth and she leaned over the banister to pull an ugly, foamy face at them. Then she darted back to the bathroom.

"Can I test Sidney out before we go off to school?" Max asked Ben.

His sister's coat was hanging invitingly on a hook near the door.

"Be my guest." Ben grinned as he

handed the spider over.

Carefully Max wedged Sidney in the cuff of the coat. Little rubber pads on the ends of the spider's legs made it nice and sticky.

Soon Jessica came pounding down the stairs, pushing past the boys. She stuck out her tongue at them and grabbed her coat. Max and Ben stood back and waited.

"**AAAARRRGHHHH!**"

"I'll save you, Jess," yelled Max over the ear-splitting screech.

He dived forward, knocked Jessica off her feet, snatched the spider and dashed out of the front door. Ben followed close behind. They skidded down the path and hid behind a bush.

"I didn't want Mum seeing Sidney," Max explained, handing the spider back to Ben. "And now I'll be a hero for rescuing Jessica from the monster. She won't pull faces at me again in a hurry."

"You think you've got it bad," said Ben. "Older sisters are worse. You should try Arabella. Mrs Hogsbum's made her a monitor at school and the power's gone to her head."

"That's dreadful!" said Max. "Better keep away from her."

Max and Ben strolled into the bustling playground.

"Let's do the spider trick again," said Ben, "before school starts." He looked around. "Who's going to scream the loudest?"

Max scanned the playground, spy radar active. He soon spotted something: clean uniforms, pink ribbons, girly giggling. He knew what that meant. Three enemy agents: Lucinda Tellingly, Poppy Parker and Tiffany Goodchild.

"I can see some likely screamers," he said. "On the bench over there."

"Brilliant," said Ben. "Tiffany's put her bag down. It's just waiting for a nice, fat, juicy spider."

Whistling innocently, the boys ambled past Tiffany and her chums. At just the right moment, Ben let Sidney fall.

"Bull's-eye!" muttered Max as the spider landed right on top of her bag.

The boys raced off to their favourite hiding place behind the bushes, and settled down to wait for the action.

"**AAARRRGHHH!**"

The ear-piercing screams of Lucinda, Poppy and Tiffany could be heard all over the school. The boys high-fived.

"My turn to be the hero," said Ben.
"I must rescue the poor girlies from the
horrible spider." He sprinted across the
playground, Max on his tail, and nearly
crashed into Miss Bleet.

"Looking for this?"
she asked, holding out
the spider between
two trembling
fingers. "I just
knew it would have
something to do with
you two. You can have

it back at lunch time. And you will be on
late lunch because you will be doing a
little job for me first."

"But it's chocolate pudding today," wailed Max. "There won't be any left by late lunch."

"Well, you can think about that while everyone else is eating and you are taking letters round to all the classrooms," said Miss Bleet. She scurried off towards the staffroom, holding the spider at arm's length.

"Teachers and girls are all the same," moaned Max. "No sense of humour."

"Greetingz!" came a growly purr from above.

The boys looked up in delight. It was Toby, their gargoyle friend. He had a huge smile on his monkey-like face and he was hanging upside down from the gutter of the roof.

"Why so grumpy?" he asked. "What's the matter?"

"Miss Bleet has taken Sidney, my super-scary, hairy spider," said Ben, pointing crossly at his teacher.

"What a mean thing to do!" said Toby. "Don't worry – I'll get it back." And he scampered away across the roof.

★ ★ ★

At playtime Max and Ben dashed outside.

"I hope Toby got Sidney back," said Max, scanning all the gutters for the gargoyle. "We've already missed out on two lessons worth of spider mischief."

"There he is," yelled Ben, pointing at the kitchen roof. "And he's got another gargoyle with him. It's one we haven't met before."

They sprinted across to the kitchen.

"I couldn't find your spider, Ben," said Toby, "even though I turned out your teacher's whole desk! This is Bartholomew, by the way."

Bartholomew was
smaller than Toby,
with wide, bulging
cheeks and pointed
ears. He had a big
round belly and
wore a pleated skirt like
a gladiator. He had a
grumpy expression on
his face. He took one look at the boys and
began to complain.

"These are humanz, Toby," he growled
in a gurgly voice. "They're not meant to
know we're alive."

"I told you about them, Bart," said
Toby. "They won't give away our secret.
Don't be such a grouch." He turned back
to the boys. "As I couldn't find your spider,
I brought Bart along instead."

"But Bart doesn't look anything *like*
a spider!" said Max.

Toby guffawed. "Of course he doesn't.

But wait till you see his special power.
Go on, Bart."

Muttering to himself, Bart clambered
down the drainpipe and squatted on the
ground. Then he opened his mouth wide
and . . . burped! It was an enormous burp,
and as it ended a huge, furry black spider
dropped out of Bart's mouth and scuttled
away across the playground.

"Wow!" exclaimed Max.

"Is it real?" gasped Ben.

The spider suddenly vanished into thin air.

"Course it's not real," Bart told them.

"My spiders don't last long and they don't hurt anybody, but they *look* real."

"That's so cool," said Max in admiration.

"And perfect for playing tricks," added Ben.

Bart stopped looking grumpy and grinned. "My record is a ten-minute tarantula," he told them.

"Could you burp up some spiders for us to take into class?" Max asked.

"My pleasure," said Bart.

Max rummaged in his rucksack and found a plastic pot. He chucked out the mouldy raisins inside and held the pot out to Bart.

Burrrrp! Arrrp! Barump!

Three hairy spiders fell into Max's pot. He put the lid on quickly.

"Thanks, Bart," he said, impressed. "We're going to have some fun with these."

Just then the bell went. Mrs Hogsbottom, the head teacher, looked very surprised to see Max and Ben running into class first.

Max waited until everyone was sitting quietly. He was on the same table as Poppy. He reached into his bag and pulled out the pot. Slowly he prised open the lid and started to tip his spiders out onto Poppy's English book ... But nothing

happened. He'd waited too long. The
spiders had gone.

At lunch time Max and Ben tried to sneak
out before Miss Bleet could give them
their punishment. But their teacher was
standing in the doorway with a pile of
papers in her hands.

"I want you to put one of these letters on every pupil's desk. It's all about a lovely trip to a sewing-machine museum." She took Sidney out of her pocket. "And you can have this back," she added. "But no more frightening Tiffany."

"We won't, miss," promised Max and Ben as they set off round the school.

"I've got a great idea," said Max when they got to the first classroom. "We don't have to go round putting a letter on every desk. Watch my incredible skill. In one clever throw I will place a letter on each chair."

He took a handful of letters and hurled them through the doorway. The letters fluttered about and floated down to land on a few chairs – and all over the floor.

"That was quick," Ben said happily. "At this rate there'll still be loads of choccy pudding left."

Five minutes later every classroom was covered in paper and Max and Ben were standing eagerly in the dinner queue.

Ben took Sidney out of his pocket. "Time for a bit of fun after all that hard work," he whispered. "We only promised not to frighten *Tiffany*. Let's try Sidney out on Duncan."

Duncan was standing in front of them. Ben put the spider on his shoulder. "Excuse

me," he said politely, "but is that a tarantula?"

Duncan looked down and saw the huge spider. "Get it off me!" he yelped, flailing about and swatting madly at Sidney.

"What's going on?" came a sharp voice.

Max looked up, his spy radar on alert: pigtails bobbing, monitor's badge gleaming, smug smile all over her face. He knew what that meant. It was Enemy Agent Arabella Neal, Ben's sister, codename: Manic Monitor.

"Oh, Ben," she said in a mock sad voice, peeling Sidney off Duncan's quivering back. "You're not still playing with that silly toy, are you? It doesn't even look real."

"Yes it *does*!" insisted Ben. "Duncan thought so."

"*I'm* the monitor here," said Arabella, sticking her nose in his face, "and it's what *I* think that counts." She smiled evilly. "I'm keeping this stupid spider and you two can go to the back of the queue."

"But that's not fair!" exclaimed Max.

"Tough!" Arabella stalked off, holding Sidney by one leg.

Max and Ben slunk to the end of the line. "They're sure to run out of chocolate pudding now," moaned Max.

"And we've lost Sidney again," said Ben, watching his sister march away.

"But that's not the worst thing," Max went on gloomily. "The worst thing is that now we'll have to eat with the monitors, because they always eat last."

"And *that* means Arabella!" groaned Ben.

Suddenly Max's face lit up. "I have a cunning plan!" he cried, and dashed away.

He got back just as Ben was being served.

"There's only one chocolate pudding left," sighed Ben.

"I don't mind," said Max. "We can share. We're going to have some fun, Agent Neal. Our mission is to sit by a window as close to Arabella as we can get."

"You're joking!" exclaimed Ben. "She'll boss us to death."

"But my plan depends on it," insisted Max.

Ben nodded, picked up his tray and zoomed across the dining hall to the table next to his sister.

Max plonked himself down beside him. "I've had a word with some *friends*," he murmured to Ben. "Now we wait for the fun to start . . ." He reached over and made sure that the window was open as wide as it would go. A moment later there was a scuffling noise, and Toby and Bart peeped over the sill.

Max held his hand under Bart's mouth.

BURRRP! A big hairy spider with red spots fell onto his palm. It was the best one yet.

"Now, do something to get Arabella's attention," Max told Ben as the spider ran up and down his arm. "And be quick. It won't last long."

"OK," said Ben, grabbing the banana from Max's tray. "Watch this, Arabella!" he called. He expertly balanced the banana on his nose and pranced up and down in front of her.

Ben's sister turned to tell him off and Max seized his chance. He reached over and carefully put the spider under a lettuce leaf on Arabella's plate.

Ben sat down again. The boys hunched over their lunches, trying not to laugh.

"**YAAAARRRGHHH!**"

Arabella leaped into the air and her plate went flying. Her friend was showered with lettuce and tomatoes.

"What's all this noise?"

"Mrs Hogsbum!" warned Max as the

head teacher loomed over them.

"There was a huge spider on my plate," whimpered Arabella. "Ben and Max put it there. They've got a trick one."

Ben put on his most innocent face. "I can't see a spider," he said. "And you took away my toy one, Arabella, even though I begged you not to." He turned sorrowful eyes on the head teacher. "It's in her pocket."

Mrs Hogsbottom glared at him suspiciously. She looked like a vulture with toothache. Out of the corner of his eye, Max saw the spider peep out from under the lettuce leaf and then disappear into thin air.

Just in time! Mrs Hogsbum examined the mess on the table with her laser vision. "I've looked through this salad," she announced, "and there is no evidence of a spider."

She frowned at Ben's sister. "You have broken school rule number forty-eight: pupils must not pretend there are spiders at the dinner table." She shook her head. "I thought you would know how to behave, Arabella Neal. If you're not careful, I will have to take back your monitor's badge." She turned on her heel and left.

Arabella threw the boys a furious look and then flounced off with her friend.

Max heard a chortling. Toby and Bart were rolling about on the window ledge.

"That's my best trick since I put spiders down the vicar's socks," said Bart.

Ben pushed the chocolate pudding over to Max and the gargoylz. "You deserve this," he said with a grin. "I don't think we'll have any more trouble from my big sister."

"Who'd have thought late lunch could turn out so well?" laughed Max, his mouth full of yummy chocolateyness.

"Dangling drainpipes!" chuckled Toby as he and Bart took mouthfuls of chocolate pudding. "You two are as mischievous as gargoylz!"

4. Now You See It, Now You Don't!

"It's Friday!" said Max as he and Ben zoomed in through the school gates on their imaginary spy spaceship. "You know what that means . . ."

"No school for two days!" yelled Ben, punching the air.

"But we won't see Toby for two days either," Max reminded him.

Ben skidded to a halt. "I didn't think of that," he said with a frown.

Max looked up at the school roof and then over to the church for their gargoyle friend. "Can't see him," he said. "That's funny. He's usually around when we get here."

"No time to find him now," said Ben as a scrawny, witch-like figure marched towards them. "Here comes Horrible Hogsbum to chase us in."

Toby didn't appear at playtime either. Max and Ben looked everywhere. They even rummaged through the PE store cupboard, where they got caught by Miss Bleet; they had to sweep it out as a punishment.

After lunch they burst into the playground.

"He's got to be somewhere," said Ben.

"Maybe he's gone on holiday or something," suggested Max.

The boys peered over the wall into the churchyard. The place was full of old grey tombstones covered in ivy.

Ben suddenly let out a cry. "There he is!"

The little monkey-faced gargoyle was sitting hunched in the long grass behind one of the tombstones. His wings were folded close to his body and he had a wicked grin on his face.

"Hey, Toby!" yelled Max, waving. "Over here!"

Toby whipped round. "*Shhhh*," he hissed. "I'm hiding from Zackary."

Max looked up and down the churchyard. "I can't see any other gargoylz," he whispered to Ben. "I think he's tricking us."

At that moment Toby was suddenly flung up into the air. He gave a yelp of surprise, somersaulted three times and landed on his bottom. Then he picked himself up and scampered over to perch on a huge stone slab near Max and Ben.

"Greetingz!" he said in his growly purr. "Zackary and I were playing hide-and-seek.

You haven't met my friend Zackary before. Say hello to my humanz, Zack." He waved a paw at the empty space beside him.

"Have you gone mad, Toby?" asked Max, scratching his head. "There's no one there."

POP! Max and Ben jumped in surprise as a grinning gargoyle appeared out of thin air. He had a fuzzy mane and a tuft on his head and he dashed up and down like an eager puppy, his eyes flashing everywhere as if he was looking for mischief.

"Morning," he said, bounding over to the boys. "Wait a sec – you're humanz. Got to be scared of humanz! Wait a sec –

you're friendly humanz. Toby told me. Nice to meet you." His words came out in a rush.

"You can make yourself invisible," gasped Ben.

"Of course!" panted Zack. "Special power." He faded in and out of view a few times. "It's easy. Can't humanz do it?"

"I wish we could," sighed Max.

"Isn't it a bit difficult to play hide-and-seek with Zack?" Ben asked Toby. "How do you ever find him?"

Toby laughed. "He's not invisible to gargoylz – only humanz."

"But how did he creep up on you like that if you can see him?" said Max.

"He's very sneaky," said Toby, "and he raced up behind me."

"I won, I won!" chanted Zack, bouncing up and down on his big floppy paws and panting loudly. "I hid the longest."

"We agreed that whoever won the game would get out of food collecting at the weekend," explained Toby.

"You did two minutes," crowed Zack, slapping Toby on the back and knocking him off the slab. "I did *twenty*."

"But that wasn't fair," protested Toby as he flew back up. "You wouldn't have known where I was if these two hadn't given the game away."

"S'pose so," grumbled Zack. "Wait a sec – call it a draw then!"

"OK, we'll both get the food tomorrow," agreed Toby. They shook paws.

"Can we help?" asked Max eagerly. "We don't have school on Saturday.

What do gargoylz eat anyway?"

"Bramblz!" said Toby.

"Thistlz!" cried Zack. "Anything with pricklz!" declared Toby in a sing-song voice. Then he added, "Rose thornz are particularly yummy, and Zack here loves stinging nettlz, don't you, Zack?"

But Zack had gone. He was bouncing over the tombstones, chanting, "Bramblz, thistlz, anything with pricklz!" as he went. He kept disappearing and then reappearing in unexpected places.

"I've got a brilliant idea!" said Max suddenly. "There are loads of brambles at the bottom of my nan's garden." Toby sat up eagerly. "We could take you and Zack there tomorrow. As long as she doesn't see you, you can get all the food you like."

"Spluttering gutterz!" exclaimed Toby. "That would be marvellous."

"You can try my nan's cupcakes as well," Max told him. "They're *her* special power!"

"Everyone loves them," agreed Ben.

Zack zoomed by at high speed. Toby
stuck out a leg, tripped him up and sat on
him. He told him Max's idea.

"And there might even be some
stingers," Max added.

"Yummmm," murmured Zack, his eyes
glazing over in delight. "Bramblz, thistlz,
anything with pricklz."

The bell rang for afternoon school.

"Oh, no!" groaned Ben. "We've got

history with Mr Oldhart now. Why do we have to have him every Friday afternoon? He's so ancient he was around with the dinosaurs. He's bound to tell us about something really boring like Stone Age soup recipes or Queen Mary's petticoats!"

"But that's not the worst thing," moaned Max. "Old Fart always gives us *loads* of homework. We won't have time to go bramble hunting at Nan's after all."

"Unless," said Ben thoughtfully, "we get Zack to make himself invisible and then rub out all the homework that Old Fart writes up on the board. We can't do any then, can we?"

"And we'd be doing him a favour really," added Max excitedly, "because he won't have all that marking on Monday!"

"You're nearly as good as gargoylz at thinking up tricks," said Toby with a sigh of admiration.

"I love tricks!" yelled Zack. "Can't wait."

"I'll get my bag," said Max, "so we can smuggle Zack into class." He raced away and was soon back with his rucksack.

Zack zoomed twice round the churchyard and leaped head first into the open bag. "Let's go!" came his muffled voice.

Max and Ben grinned at each other. This was going to be a great trick!

The two boys made their way into class and sat at a table right underneath Mr Oldhart's nose. Max made sure he put his bag down out of sight.

"I don't like it at the front," Ben whispered with a shudder. "Gives me the heebie-jeebies."

Mr Oldhart put a pile of grey books down on his desk. He arranged his pens in a circle around his glasses case and blew his nose loudly. Then he began to drone on. Max and Ben watched the hands of the clock tick slowly round.

"This is the most boring history lesson in the history of boring history lessons," muttered Max, his head in his hands. "Who cares about basket weaving in the Middle Ages?"

"And we're too near Old Fart to have

a pencil fight," groaned Ben. "Or even a rubber-flicking contest."

"Now, class, the moment you've all been waiting for," announced Mr Oldhart at last, his eyes gleaming. "I'm going to

write your homework instructions on the board for you to copy down. While I'm doing it, I want you to draw a picture of the wicker basket on page eleven. I know you're all eager, but take your time. One should never rush a picture of a wicker basket."

Max sprang into action. He knocked his pencil to the floor and stuck his head under the table, pretending to look for it. "Get ready, Zack!" he whispered into his rucksack.

There was a shuffling noise and a fuzzy mane appeared.

"You're supposed to be invisible!" Max reminded the excited gargoyle. There was a faint **pop** and Zack vanished.

Mr Oldhart filled the board with homework and turned back to the class. "I've given you plenty to keep you busy till Monday," he said happily. "I wouldn't want you getting bored over the weekend."

The class read the instructions, realized there would be hours of work, and groaned.

"I knew you'd be pleased." Mr Oldhart beamed.

"Go, Zack!" whispered Max.

Very soon every trace of homework had disappeared, wiped away by an invisible paw. Max and Ben could hardly keep straight faces; their classmates couldn't keep straight faces at all. They were soon laughing and pointing at the blank whiteboard.

"Oh, no!" groaned Ben. "He'll see what's happened before it's time to go home."

Mr Oldhart turned to the board. He took off his glasses and rubbed his eyes. "I could have sworn I put the homework up there just now," he muttered.

He sighed and wrote it up for a second time, but as soon as he turned back to his

table, the words disappeared again. This time everyone except Max and Ben was busily copying the picture of the basket, so they didn't notice. Max held his breath. Perhaps Old Fart wouldn't notice that the homework had vanished either. But, to his dismay, their teacher suddenly swung round to the board.

"I quite forgot to put up question twenty-three . . ." he murmured. Then he stopped and stared at the board in disbelief. "Who did that?" he demanded.

"Did what, sir?" asked Ben innocently.

"Someone has rubbed the homework off the board," Mr Oldhart said, peering suspiciously at Ben and Max. "Mrs Hogsbottom warned me about you two.

Have you boys got something to do
with this?"

"Not us, sir," said Max. "We haven't left
our chairs."

Mr Oldhart sighed deeply and turned
back to the board. He wrote all the
homework up for a third time and then
sat and watched the class closely.

"This isn't working," whispered Ben.
"How can we stop him from noticing
the empty board when Zack rubs out
the writing?"

"Hmm . . ." Max murmured.
Then, "Got it!"
he whispered.
He bent down
and pretended to
get something
out of his bag.
"Zack!" he said softly.
"This time, can you
write different words

up there instead, so that Old Fart won't see an empty board? You can write, can't you?"

Zack stuck his head out eagerly. "Course I can, silly human!"

"Then give us some really fun homework," said Max.

"With plenty of football," added Ben.

POP! Zack disappeared.

And a few seconds later, so did the writing on the board.

Max looked around. Everyone had their heads bent over their books. Mr Oldhart was still glaring at the class. Max glanced back at the board. To his delight, new words were being scribbled all over it, but then he realized that he could see something else too . . .

"Oh, no!" he muttered to Ben. "Zack's tail has appeared!"

Ben looked up. Now the boys could see little claws and the hint of a mane.

"As soon as you've finished your
picture, you can copy down the homework
instructions," Mr Oldhart told the class.
A worried look crossed his face and he
turned to glance at the board. Max caught
his breath nervously, but, in the nick of
time, Zack skittered away from the board

and threw himself into the rucksack. Mr Oldhart looked back at the class, clearly satisfied that the homework was still there for all to see.

"He didn't notice that the words are different," whispered Max.

"Better do as he says then," grinned Ben.

Along with the rest of the class, the boys grabbed their pencils and carefully wrote down – *'Play lots of football, hide-and-seek and pranks. Have lots of fun!'*

The bell rang. School was over for another week. Everyone in the class grabbed their bags and ran out of the room, giggling at Mr Oldhart's surprising choice of homework. Max made sure Zack was safely inside his rucksack and then made a bolt for the door, Ben at his heels.

"Football? Hide-and-seek? *Pranks?*" they heard Mr Oldhart splutter as they dashed out of the classroom. He had finally read the board.

The boys had just escaped round the corner when a dreadful figure loomed up in front of them. It was Mrs Hogsbottom.

"Uh-oh!" muttered Max. "Do you think she can have found out about the homework?"

Mrs Hogsbottom planted herself in front of the boys, one hand behind her back. "Aren't you forgetting something, Ben?" she boomed.

"Er . . . no . . . It wasn't us who . . ." stammered Ben.

"Rule seven," said Mrs Hogsbottom, producing Ben's football from behind her back. "Head teachers always return footballs when they say they will."

"Thanks Mrs Hogsbu— ttom!" said Ben, grabbing it.

Outside in the playground, Max and Ben sprinted across to the wall by the churchyard. Making sure that no one was looking, Max put down his bag and let Zack out. The little gargoyle scampered over the wall, where Toby was waiting to hear all about it.

Zack told him what had happened – acting out the best bits all around the churchyard.

When he'd finished, Toby patted him on the head. "That's the best trick you've played since you juggled the hymn books and frightened the vicar," he said proudly. Then he waggled a finger at Max and Ben.

"You two had better go home and get on with that homework!"

"We'll start right now," said Ben seriously, and he spun his football on one finger.

"And tomorrow we'll take you to Nan's and give you your treat," added Max.

"Bramblz, thistlz, anything with pricklz!" yelled Zack. "You should try them too!"

The boys laughed.

"I think we'll stick to Nan's cupcakes, thanks," Max said with a grin.

Book Two:
Gargoylz Get Up to Mischief!

1. Gnome, Sweet Gnome

It was Saturday morning. Nine-year-old Max Black zoomed along in his imaginary spy car and screeched to a halt outside Oldacre Primary School. His best friend Ben was waiting for him.

"I can't believe we're at school at the weekend!" said Max.

"Neither can I." Ben grinned at him. "But at least we're not going in."

"You're right," said Max. "Ready for our new mission, Agent Neal?"

"Of course," said Ben. "Secret Plan: Take the Gargoylz to Your Nan's. But where are

119

Toby and Zack? They said they'd meet us here. We can't go without them."

"Greetingz!" came a growly purr from the graveyard and a small creature flew up onto the churchyard wall.

Max activated his spy radar to check him out: monkey face, pointy ears, stony skin. He knew what that meant. It was Toby, their gargoyle friend.

Max and Ben had a big secret. The gargoylz that hung on the ancient church next to their school were not the stone statues that everyone thought they were.

They were alive. And they'd made friends
with Max and Ben. Like the boys, the
gargoylz enjoyed having fun and playing
tricks. It was a perfect partnership!

Toby wagged his pointy tail at the boys.
"Ready for bramble collecting?" he asked
as he fluttered his leafy wings and
flew over to perch on Max's
shoulder. All gargoylz
had a special power
and Toby's was flying.
Although lots of the
gargoylz had wings,
Toby was the only
one the boys had
met who could use
them to actually fly.

This weekend Toby
and Zack were on bramble-collecting duty
for all the other gargoylz. Prickly plants
were their favourite food, and Max knew
exactly where they could get plenty of

those – his nan's garden.

"We brought our rucksacks so that you can hide inside them," said Max. "You mustn't be seen trotting along the high street."

"Quite right!" declared Toby. He flew into Ben's bag and popped his head out of the top. "Well, what are we waiting for? I want to get my pawz on those thorny snacks."

"And I want to get my hands on Nan's cupcakes," said Max. "Best things in the world."

"We can't go without Zack," said Ben, looking around. "Where is he?"

"Bramblz, thistlz, anything with pricklz!" came a cheeky voice beside him.

There was no one to be seen.

"Invisible again, Zack?" Max laughed.

POP! A gargoyle with a fuzzy mane and a tuft on his head appeared on the wall. He zipped up and down and then sat there panting, his tongue hanging out. "No bag for me," he declared, looking at Max's open rucksack. "I'll disappear instead. My special gargoyle power. Won't be seen."

"Yes you will," said Ben. "You're always appearing when you don't mean to."

"Good point," chortled Zack.

He hopped into Max's rucksack. "Come on. I'm hungry."

"Hold on tight," yelled Max, zooming off at top speed. "We're using our spy car and it's really fast."

Two minutes later they were knocking on a bright blue door. It opened. Max checked his spy radar: curly hair, big smile, apron covered in flour. It was Nan, codename: Supercook.

"Hello, dears." She beamed as the boys followed her towards the kitchen. "You're just in time. I've been baking."

Ben's rucksack gave a shake.

"Spluttering gutterz!" came a growly voice from inside. "Smellz delicious."

"Glad you think so, Ben," replied Nan as they followed her into the kitchen. "But what's happened to your voice? It sounds as if you've got a cold. I'll give you some of my special cure later."

"Thanks, Mrs Black," said Ben politely, nudging his rucksack with his elbow to keep Toby quiet.

Max made a face at his friend. Nan might be the best cupcake maker in the world but her homemade medicines were foul.

Nan opened the back door. "Now why don't you go and play in the garden like

175

you usually do, and I'll bring some freshly baked cupcakes out in a little while."

The boys grinned and raced across the lawn to the bottom of the garden where Nan's blackberry bushes grew in a weedy tangle. They were hidden from the rest of the garden by an apple tree and some rhododendrons. Max and Ben opened their rucksacks and let the gargoylz out.

"What a feast!" gasped Toby, his eyes

on stalks at the sight of the brambles and nettles.

"Let me at 'em!" cried Zack, diving straight into the thorns.

"Wait for me," called Toby, flapping his wings and zooming in after him.

"We'll help you pick them," said Max. "I've got top secret spy gloves." He pulled them out of his rucksack. "They're my dad's best ones. I had to sneak them out.

They're brand new so they're sure to be prickle-proof."

"And I've got special agent bramble slicers," said Ben, waving a pair of scissors. "They're my sister's. She uses them for her scrapbook. She'd explode if she knew I had them. You hold the brambles and I'll cut them."

Max and Ben soon had a big pile of bramble stalks by their feet. Suddenly it began to heave and wobble as if it was alive. Then Toby's head popped out, scattering branches and leaves everywhere.

"Tasty bramblz," he said, with his mouth full. "You two are wonderful collectors."

Max laughed. "How many have you collected? Don't forget you two are supposed to be picking them for all the

other gargoylz as well. You're not meant to eat them all."

Toby looked sheepish. "But they're so delicious."

POP! A dragony tail appeared beside him followed by the rest of Zack. "Best place for pricklz ever," he said, munching away.

"Coo-ee, boys!"

"Hide!" whispered Max. "It's Nan. She mustn't see you."

ZOOM! ZOOM! Zack and Toby jumped out of the bramble pile and dived headfirst into the bushes just as Nan

appeared with a tray. She set it down on the grass.

"I've brought you some juice and cupcakes. I wasn't sure which toppings you'd like so there's a selection."

"Thanks, Nan," said Max, eyeing the huge pile of brightly coloured iced cakes in delight.

There was a rustling in the bushes followed by a licking of stone lips, and a pair of stone ears suddenly popped up.

Nan frowned. "I hope that's not a cat in my blackberries," she muttered.

"A cat?" came Toby's indignant growl from the bush.

"Ben dear," said Nan. "Your voice is getting worse. I'm going straight back in to make some of my special cold cure."

She suddenly noticed the pile of brambles. "What do you want those for?" she asked.

"Er . . . they're for the school rabbit," said Max quickly.

"Yes . . . he's staying at my house for the weekend," added Ben.

Nan looked puzzled. "They're a bit prickly for a rabbit, aren't they?"

"It's . . . it's . . . a very rare rabbit," said

Max. "Isn't it, Ben?"

"Yes. It's a . . . er . . . Bramble-eating Stony Church Rabbit," gabbled Ben. "It loves prickly things."

"Well, fancy that." Nan turned to go back into the house. "Enjoy your cakes."

As soon as she'd gone the gargoylz scampered out.

"Cat indeed!" exclaimed Toby. "Ferocious yowling creatures with too much fur—" He suddenly saw the cupcakes. "Are these like the cookiez I had at school?" he asked eagerly. "I love cookiez."

"They're the cupcakes I told you

about," said Max, holding out the plate. "Try one."

Toby stretched out a paw and grabbed a cake, then stuffed it in his mouth. "Dangling drainpipes, they're delicious!" he sighed happily.

"Let me try! Let me try!" Zack cried, gobbling up a cake and grabbing two more – one in each paw. He darted off, sat down in the weeds and munched noisily.

Three minutes later every cake had gone. Both gargoylz lay on the grass, bellies bulging.

"Shame there aren't any more," said Toby.

"You've had ten!" Max exclaimed.

"Ben and I were lucky to get any once you two started!"

"Coo-ee," came Nan's voice. "I've brought a bag for the brambles – and my special cold cure for you, Ben."

POP! Zack vanished. Toby struggled to his feet but he didn't have time to hide. He was stranded on the grass in full view. He froze, a horrified expression on his face, as Nan appeared holding out a mug of bubbling green liquid. It smelled like old socks.

She spotted Toby immediately. "What a lovely little garden gnome!" she said, putting the mug down on the grass and giving him a poke. "Did you make him at school, Max?"

"No . . . er . . . yes," said Max. How was

he going to get Toby out of this?

"Look at his diddy little hands and his little round tummy," Nan went on. "He'd look lovely in my rockery."

"I can't let you keep him, Nan," said Max hurriedly. "He's got to go back to the chur— I mean, school. He's not finished."

"I can see that now," said his grandmother kindly. "His face looks ever so ugly."

There was a growly snort of laughter in the air behind them from Zack.

Nan looked anxiously at Ben. "You still don't sound right, dear," she said. "Drink up your medicine like a good boy."

"Er . . ." quavered Ben, bending down to pick up the revolting drink.

Max could see his friend needed a

137

plan – Operation Spill the Drink. But before he could do anything there was a faint slurping noise from the mug. The boys gazed down in astonishment as the bubbling green liquid quickly disappeared. Max hid a grin. Invisible Zack must have sneaked out of the bushes. Luckily Nan didn't seem to have noticed.

Ben swept up the empty mug and pretended to drink the mixture down in one gulp. "Thanks." He grinned. "It was . . . tasty."

An almighty gargoyle burp filled the air. "Pardon me!" said Ben quickly.

"My cure never fails," chirped Nan. "See, your voice is back to normal already." She bent down and patted Toby on the head. "And I've got the very thing for you, Mr Gnome. I'll be back in a jiffy."

She bustled off to the house. Max and Ben burst out laughing.

POP! Zack appeared, wiping green goo off his chin. "Sorry, Ben. Drank it all. Couldn't resist. Nearly as tasty as bramblz." He raced over to Toby. "Mr Gnome!" he giggled, skipping around him. "Mr Gnome!"

Toby looked furious. "Mr Gnome!" he spluttered, jumping to his feet. "I'm an ancient stone gargoyle who's lived proudly on the church for more than eight hundred yearz and your nan thinks I'm a garden ornament!"

"Ugly garden ornament!" chuckled Zack, rolling on his back and kicking his legs in the air.

"Coo-ee!" Nan was suddenly back, waving something small and red.

POP! Zack disappeared. Toby froze again.

"All garden gnomes should have one of these," she said.

Max and Ben tried desperately not to laugh as Nan carefully fitted a pointy, red woolly hat over Toby's monkey ears.

"How sweet!" She beamed, tickling him under the chin. "Who's a smart Mr Gnome then?"

Max suddenly realized he could see a
tail appearing on the grass in front of him .
. . then a paw . . . then an ear . . . Zack was
forgetting to stay invisible. Max stepped
smartly in front of him but it was too late.

"What's that behind you, dear?" asked
Nan, peering round him. Zack was
completely visible now. "Oh, you didn't
tell me there was a little girly one as well!"
she exclaimed. "Did you make her, Ben?
She's so sweet!" Nan patted Zack's fuzzy
stone mane. "You've even tried to give her

some hair." She reached into her apron pocket and pulled out a lacy handkerchief. "I haven't got another hat," she explained, "but this will do nicely." She fixed the hankie round Zack's head like a scarf and tied it under his chin. "Mr and Mrs Gnome. What a lovely couple!"

"Thanks, Nan," gulped Max. He had to get away before he burst out laughing. "We have to be off now. Back to Ben's house. To give the rabbit its lunch."

"Yes, you get along and give that Stony Church thingamabob a real treat," agreed Nan, helping the boys to put the brambles into the bag. While her back was turned Max beckoned to the gargoylz. They hopped into the rucksacks.

"I'll see you soon," Nan called, waving the boys off from the garden gate.

SECRET CODEWORD:
PLOT

Max and Ben reached the church
wall and opened their bags. The gargoylz
tumbled out and Max handed Toby the
bag of brambles.

"Let's go home, Mr Gnome!" Zack
laughed.

"All right, Mrs Gnome," answered Toby.
"Little girly one!"

"Hmph!" snorted Zack. "Make a pact.
No more gnome talk."

"Agreed," said Toby as they scampered
off and the boys headed home. "But it was
funny when she called you a girl. I haven't
laughed so much since I put nettlz in the
vicar's breakfast."

2. Kitten Caper

Secret Agent Max Black strolled along the road on his way to school. He heard the sound of wheels racing over the pavement and turned on his spy radar: blond hair, blue eyes, battered knee pads. It was Agent Ben Neal, riding a gleaming new skateboard.

"Awesome!" Max exclaimed as Ben stopped and flipped the shiny red board into his hand. "That's the Speed King!"

"It's new," said Ben proudly. "I've brought it to show everyone this afternoon when all the Year Four classes get together to do Hobbies Talk."

They ran through the school gates.

"Greetingz!"

The monkey face of a cheeky gargoyle was hanging down from the school roof.

Max beamed. "Hello there, Toby." Then he spotted something on the roof behind him. Something small and fluffy. "There's a kitten stuck up there!" he gasped, pointing.

"Poor thing," said Ben. "Can you rescue it, Toby?"

To their surprise Toby burst out laughing. "Spluttering gutterz!" he guffawed. "That's not a kitten. That's my gargoyle friend Theophilus. His special power is meant to be turning into a ferocious tiger but it never works. Theo, say hello to Max and Ben."

As they watched, the tabby ball of fluff gave a determined **miaow**. After a lot of wriggling it slowly changed shape until a gargoyle sat in its place.

The new gargoyle had a long, tigerish tail and his golden stone was slightly stripy. His face was a bit like a cat's,

with bristling whiskers and small, friendly-looking fangs. He stared at Max and Ben.

"Humanz!" he gasped with an anxious swish of his tail. "Help! They mustn't see us."

"It's OK, Theo." Toby laughed. "These two are my friends. They'll keep our secret."

"That's all right then." Theo beamed at Max and Ben. "Sorry if I frightened you when I was a ferocious tiger."

"You weren't exactly ferocious . . ." began Max.

"Wasn't I?" said Theo.

"And you weren't exactly a tiger," Ben told him.

"Wasn't I?" sighed Theo.

"More of a kitten really," explained Max with an apologetic grin.

"Oh dear," said Theo dejectedly. "I was so sure I'd become a tiger this time. The thing is, I'm only four hundred and twelve

148

years old. I haven't had long to practise."

"You were a very good kitten," Max reassured him.

"Keep practising and you'll be the most ferocious tiger in the world," said Toby. "It'll only take another hundred years or so." He caught sight of the Speed King. "What's that?"

"It's my new skateboard," said Ben, holding it up for him to see.

"New board?" came a harsh voice behind them. Toby and Theo froze into statues.

Max's spy radar picked up trouble: shaved head, big fists,  sticky-out ears. He knew what that meant.

It was Enemy Agent Barry Price, also known as The Basher, codename: School Bully.

SPY FILE:

Codename:
School
Bully

The next minute The Basher had Ben's skateboard in his hands.

"Give it back, Barry!" Ben pleaded. "You can have a look at it this afternoon when our classes get together."

"No one'll want to see this rubbish," scoffed The Basher. "Not when I show them what I've brought." He tapped his school bag with a gloating grin.

"What *have* you brought then?" asked Max.

"It's a secret," Barry said, and, to their horror, jumped on Ben's skateboard. "See you later!"

He streaked off across the playground,
whooping triumphantly and bashing kids
over as he went.

Suddenly Max saw a tall figure emerging from the school door. Grey hair, beaky nose, face like thunder. He knew what that meant. It was Enemy Agent Mrs Hogsbottom, commonly known as Mrs Hogsbum, codename: Stinky Head Teacher. The Basher zoomed past the door and went **smack!** straight into her, knocking her right off her feet.

"Outrageous!" shrieked Mrs Hogsbottom, staggering up again and staring at Barry with her laser vision. "School rule number twenty-seven. The head teacher must not be run over without permission. I shall keep this

monstrosity until home time."

"I never thought I'd say this," gasped Max, "but Mrs Hogsbum's done us a favour. She's taken the Speed King off The Basher for us."

"I'll go and get it back," said Ben eagerly.

The boys rushed over to the furious head teacher, who was brushing gravel off her bony knees. The Basher stood smirking behind her.

"What do you two want?" she snapped as soon as she saw them.

"The skateboard's mine, Mrs Hogsbottom," Ben began to explain. "Could I have it back please?"

"Certainly not!" sniffed the head teacher. "If you hadn't

lent it to Barry Price this wouldn't have
happened."

"I didn't lend it," said Ben. "He snatched
it." He put on his wide-eyed, pleading
look. It always worked on the dinner
ladies, who gave him extra pudding. It
never worked on Mrs Hogsbottom.

"No excuses," she snapped, picking
up the Speed King and tucking it firmly
under her arm.

"But Ben has to show it to everyone in

class later," pleaded Max. "He brought it in specially for the talk."

"Ben should have thought of that when he lent it to Barry Price," said Mrs Hogsbottom crossly. "He can have it back after school." She turned on her heel and marched towards the door.

The Basher poked his face into Ben's.

"What a shame!" he sniggered.

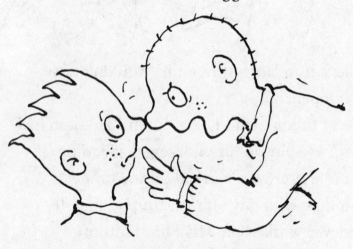

"Still, never mind. No one would have listened to you whingeing on about skateboarding. My hobby's much better."

He strutted off, pushing a couple of

small footballers out of the way as he went.

"I don't reckon he's got anything better than your Speed King," said Max when The Basher was out of earshot.

"At least he's got *something*," sighed Ben miserably.

"That was really mean," came a growly purr. Toby was watching The Basher go. "Wish I had my catapult with me. I'd fire some acorns at him."

"When he comes back I'm going to turn into a tiger," said Theo. He stretched out a front paw. Three tiny claws appeared. "That'll give him a scare."

The bell rang. Mrs Hogsbottom stood by the door, fuming.

"We'd better go in," sighed Max, "before she explodes."

"That was the worst morning in the history of worst mornings," said Ben at lunch time. "We haven't played a trick on anyone."

"We've been too busy thinking about how to get our own back on The Basher," Max pointed out.

"And my poor Speed King is being held prisoner," said Ben. "Mrs Hogsbum is probably feeding it to her crocodiles right now."

Max's eyes suddenly lit up. "Don't despair, Agent Neal," he said. "We'll do a great trick and get our own back at the same time." He leaned forward to whisper in Ben's ear, "Barry's got something in his bag that he reckons is really cool, right?"

Ben nodded. "Right, Agent Black."

"Then our mission is to swap it for something stupid and girly." Max grinned. "When he gets it out to show everyone he'll be dead embarrassed."

"Good plan!" breathed Ben. "And I know just the thing – my sister Arabella's ballet tutu. It's all pink and frilly and

161

horrible. It's in her ballet bag. Only one problem," he added with a frown. "The bag is in the girls' cloakroom and boys are not allowed in there. If we get caught we'll never hear the end of it."

"I know someone who can help us with that!" said Max, nodding up at the roof.

"Toby!" exclaimed Ben as their  gargoyle friend waved at them from a gutter. "He could fly in through the cloakroom window and get it for us, no problem."

Making sure no one was looking, the boys sauntered over towards Toby.

"Greetingz!" called Toby chirpily.

"Hi, Toby," Max called back. "Want to help with a trick?"

Toby's yellow eyes lit up and his dragon tail swished. "A trick?" he said eagerly. "A prank? Dangling drainpipes! Tell me all about it!"

Max gave Toby his instructions for Secret Plan: Tutu. Chuckling, the little gargoyle zoomed off to the girls' cloakroom window. In a flash he was back with Arabella's pink tutu in his paws.

"I can hardly bear to touch it, it's so girly," declared Max, pulling a disgusted face. "It's lucky all the school rucksacks look the same. We'll swap my bag for Barry's." He stuffed the tutu in his bag.

"There's one thing we haven't thought of," said Ben. "How are we going to stop The Basher seeing when we swap them round? It's not much of a trick if he catches us at it!"

"Can I join in?" Theo's stripy head popped up over the gutter. "Maybe I'll manage a tiger this time."

"No, we need a kitten," cried Ben, "for Secret Plan: Kitten Diversion. Agent Black, do you remember when that big black cat jumped through the window of our classroom last term? Everyone went all gooey and Miss Bleet forgot to give us any maths homework. Think what would happen if a sweet little tabby kitten came in instead. No one would see us making the bag switch then."

"I like your thinking, Agent Neal," said Max. "Listen, Theo, we've got a trick to play this afternoon and we need everyone to be looking at you while we're setting it up."

A broad grin spread over Theo's whiskery face. "What do I have to do?" he asked, almost falling off the roof in excitement.

"We need you to come in through our classroom window this afternoon," said Max. "While everyone's looking at you, we'll swap The Basher's bag with the one that has the frilly pink tutu in it. All the class will laugh when he gets it out."

"Serve the bully right," said Toby.

"I can do that!" cried Theo.

Just then the bell rang.

"Right!" said Max. "I'll leave a window open for you this afternoon. Come in as soon as we start the lesson. When we've swapped the bags, I'll say the password and you can skedaddle."

"Yes, sir!" Theo sat up proudly. "What's the password?"

"Tiddles," said Max.

Straight after register it was time for Hobbies Talk. The other class in their year group came in, led by Barry.

"Shove up!" he said nastily, pushing a row of girls out of the way.

"Quick," Max whispered to Ben. "Go and grab us a couple of seats behind The Basher. I'll open a window. I hope Theo remembers what to do."

Max joined Ben in the row behind the bully. Barry turned and smirked at the boys.

"I'm looking forward to your talk, Ben," he sneered. "What's it about? Oh yes, I remember. Nothing!"

"Quiet please," came a quavery voice. Max's spy radar snapped into action:

short and dumpy, limp brown hair, silly half-moon glasses. It was Enemy Agent Miss Bleet, codename: Wimpy Teacher.

"Welcome to Hobbies Talk," Miss Bleet said feebly. "Lucinda, you start."

There was a groan as Lucinda Tellingly marched up to the front clutching her huge collection of plastic ponies.

"I hope Theo comes in soon," muttered Max. "I can't bear to hear much of this."

"These are my special horses," Lucinda began to coo. "They all have names and— Oooh, look at the darling kitten!"

Everyone turned to where she was pointing. Theo, in his cutest tabby form, was perched on the window ledge. He jumped into the room and darted about, as if he was chasing imaginary mice.

"Here, sweetums!" cooed Miss Bleet, bending down. Theo rubbed round her ankles and purred.

"Now's our chance," hissed Max. "All eyes are on Theo, even The Basher's!"

"Ready for synchronized bag switching?" asked Ben.

Max nodded. Ben reached under Barry's chair and snatched up the Basher's bag. Max put his own in its place. Then they both sat back and looked innocent.

"Tiddles!" Max called. Everyone stared at him in astonishment. "Er . . . I recognize the cat . . . He's called Tiddles and he lives down my road," Max explained with a shrug.

But Theo didn't take his cue and jump out of the window. He was having too much fun. He was now sitting on Miss Bleet's table, playing with her pencil.

"Tiddles!" said Max loudly.

Theo let go of the pencil but rolled over onto his back, looking adorable and knocking Miss Bleet's papers to the floor.

"We won't have time for the trick at this rate," Ben muttered to Max.

"TIDDLES!" yelled Max.

Theo scrambled to his feet and bolted out of the window with a loud **miaow**.

171

"How mean!" said Lucinda, glaring at Max. "Scaring the poor little thing like that."

"Quiet please," said Miss Bleet, in a fluster. "The cat's gone. Who'd like to go next?"

"But I haven't—" began Lucinda.

"Me!" interrupted Barry Price, grabbing the bag under his chair and marching to the front. "You won't want to listen to anyone else after my go. I've got the best hobby in the world!" He delved into his bag. "Every Saturday I wear this." He pulled out the pink tutu and held it up proudly.

For a long moment there was a shocked silence in the class and then everyone burst out laughing. The Basher suddenly realized what he was holding. He stared at the tutu as if it was a poisonous snake.

"This isn't mine!" he yelled, flinging it to the floor. "Where's my crash helmet? That's what I was going to show you. I do go-karting every weekend."

"You shouldn't be ashamed of enjoying ballet, Barry," said Miss Bleet kindly. "We'd all like to hear about it, wouldn't we, class?"

"YES!" The shout echoed around the room.

"But I don't do ballet!" Barry made his way back to his place, his face bright red.

"It's girly. I told you: I do go-karting."

Miss Bleet wasn't listening. "Now tell us all about why you choose to wear a tutu."

"I DON'T WEAR A STUPID TUTU!"

The Basher slumped down in his seat, glaring at everyone. He didn't say another word for the rest of the day. He didn't even notice when Max swapped the bags back.

As soon as the bell rang, Max and Ben dashed off to Mrs Hogsbottom's office to retrieve the Speed King.

"School Rule number four hundred and seventeen," she barked as soon as she saw them. "Boys must not dash into the head teacher's office to get their skateboards back. School rule two hundred and fifty-five . . ."

175

Five school rules later they were finally released. They ran to the school gate.

"Did you see The Basher's face when he realized what he was holding?" chuckled Ben. "Imagine him go-karting in a tutu!"

"Oh no! Your sister's tutu!" gasped Max. "It's still on the classroom floor!"

Ben turned white. "We're in big trouble. Come on, we've got to get it back without being seen."

They were just heading back towards the school door when something fell on

Ben's head. It was pink and frilly. Max looked up to see Toby on the school roof, with Theo next to him.

"That was a great trick you played on The Basher!" wheezed Toby as Ben struggled with the tutu on his head. "I haven't laughed so much since Theo chased a mouse up the vicar's trousers."

"Thanks, Toby." Max grinned. "And thanks, Theo – you were an awesome kitten."

"You wait till you see my tiger," said Theo. "Only another hundred years and I'll get it perfect."

Ben emerged from under the tutu. "If you go and put this back in Arabella's bag

for me," he said, putting his skateboard on
the ground, "I'll give you both a ride on
my Speed King."

"Spluttering gutterz!" the gargoylz
shouted together, grabbing the tutu and
rushing off with it.

3. Toby Stows Away

Max and Ben jumped up from their seats. School was over for another day.

"I thought that maths lesson would never end," complained Max, grabbing his bag.

"It must have been about a hundred years long," agreed Ben. They made a dash for the classroom door.

"Freedom awaits!" yelled Max as they sped along the corridor and out into the playground. "And we've got important people to see."

"Important gargoylz!" Ben grinned.

They sprinted across to peer over the church wall.

"Hello," said a shy voice, and Barney's doggy face peeped round a gravestone. "Pleased to see you."

He began to waddle towards the boys when all of a sudden he jolted forward and rolled over and over. The spikes on his back stuck out, making him look like a hedgehog.

POP! Zach appeared out of thin air by his side, his fuzzy mane quivering around his face. "Sorry, Barney!" he cried.

"Bumped into you. Wasn't looking." **POP!**
He vanished again.

"Where's Toby?" asked Max.

"I don't know," said Barney, looking around. "He was here a minute ago."

A window creaked open on the other side of the playground.

"Outrageous!" came a harsh voice.

Max spun round. It was Mrs Hogsbottom.

"School rule number three hundred and eighty-two," she screeched across the playground. "Boys must not talk to the wall! Get yourselves home, NOW!"

"Yes, Mrs Hogsbottom," they called.

"We've got to go," Max hissed to Barney. "See you tomorrow."

Barney gave them a cheery wave and

then crouched back down behind the gravestone. He put a paw to his lips. "Shhh!" he warned. "I'm going to jump out on Zack – if I'm fast enough."

Max and Ben set off home. "I hope Barney remembers not to make any of his special disgusting smells," said Ben. "Zack will know where he is at once."

Max hoisted his school bag onto his shoulders. "I wonder where Toby was."

"Probably playing a trick on the vicar," said Ben. "Come on, Agent Black, all aboard our Secret Agent Speedboat."

They zoomed off home.

Max burst through his back door into the kitchen and dropped his bag on the floor. There was someone at the table. He

activated his spy
radar: dark brown
hair, red jumper,
potato peeler in
hand. It was Mrs
Joanne Black,
codename: Mum.

"I'm starving!"
gasped Max,
clutching his stomach.
He grabbed a packet of biscuits, ran into
the hall and made for the stairs. "Can I
have one?" he yelled over his shoulder.

"You can have one and one only,"
called Mum. "I don't want you spoiling
your dinner. And don't leave your bag
down here for me to fall over. Come back
and take it up to your bedroom."

Max had reached the top of the stairs.
He looked at the packet of biscuits and
sighed. He'd have to get his school bag
or his mother would keep on nagging.

With a clever spin, he was back down in the kitchen before she could say tidy up. He swung his bag over his shoulder, raced upstairs and flung it on the bed.

Then he sat on the floor, ready to eat his biscuit.

"Mum just doesn't understand a boy's stomach," he groaned as he pulled out one chocolate digestive. "This will disappear into the empty void. I could eat the whole packet and still have room for dinner – except peas. There'd be no room for peas."

"Greetingz!" came a voice from his bag. "What are peas?"

Max whipped round. Something was clambering out of his bag. His spy radar homed in: monkey face, pointy ears, cheeky smile. It was Toby, codename: Gargoyle Friend.

"Toby!" Max exclaimed. "Awesome. We can play all evening."

"Is that a cookie?" asked the gargoyle,

scrambling over and sniffing the packet.

"Yes," said Max. "These are chocolate digestives. They're delicious. Try one."

He handed Toby the biscuits. Mum had said he could only have one. That didn't mean Toby couldn't have one as well.

Max finished his and dived under his bed. "I've got something to show you," he called. At last he reappeared, empty-handed, his hair standing even more on end than usual. "Well, I will have when I find it. It's my remote-control car. I thought it was under the bed but there are only spiders there." He rummaged in a box of action figures, then threw all the shoes

out of his wardrobe. He emptied a drawer
onto a mountain of socks and underpants.
"Got it!" he cried at last, holding out a
shiny sports car. "You can have first go.
You just switch it
on and—"

He gawped.
Toby's monkey
face was covered in
chocolate and the
empty biscuit packet
was scrunched up
in his paw. He was
smiling blissfully.

"You've eaten the lot!" Max gasped.
"Mum'll think it was me. I'm going to be
in big trouble."

Toby looked worried. "Sorry, Max,"
he said. "I couldn't help myself. You were
right. They're delicious."

Max jumped to his feet. "I've had a
brainwave!" he said. "I'll sneak the packet

downstairs and put it in the cupboard.
Hopefully, Mum will think my sister Jessica
has eaten them all! Stay here. It won't
take me long to carry out my new secret
mission."

Agent Max Black crept down the stairs
and along the hall. The television was on
and he could see Enemy Agents Mum and
Jessica watching it. They were no match
for a superspy like him. He sneaked past

unseen and opened the kitchen door, making sure that it didn't creak. Then he skidded across to the cupboard. He reached up to put the empty packet back on the shelf.

"Max!" His mum was right behind him. He hadn't heard her. She must be wearing her special Enemy Agent Stealth Slippers. "What are you doing?" She saw the empty packet in his hand. "Have you eaten all the biscuits?"

"No!" said Max truthfully. "I only had one like you said."

"And I suppose the fairies had the rest," sighed his mother. "You'd better eat all your dinner."

"I will!"

"I'm giving you extra peas," she went on. "Now go up to the bathroom and wash your hands before you eat."

Max escaped.

He wasn't going to bother to wash his

hands. They weren't that dirty. He'd only made one mud pie at lunch time. Instead he dashed up to see Toby again.

"I've got to have my dinner now," he told him. "You must stay here until I get back. And no more trouble!"

"I'll be good," said Toby, looking around the room. "Lots for me to do."

"Max!" shouted his mum. "Dinner's on the table."

Mum doled out the apple crumble and handed it round. Max poured custard over it and tucked in. It was his favourite pudding.

Plop! A large drop of water splashed into his bowl. Then another.

Dad leaped to his feet. "We've got a leak!" he cried, pointing up at the ceiling, where a damp patch was spreading.

"Did you forget to turn the tap off, Max?" demanded Mum.

Max shook his head, but he had a nasty feeling he might know who did . . .

"Don't worry," he yelled as he charged down the hall. "I'll see to it."

He took the stairs two at a time and flung the bathroom door open. His jaw dropped in horror. The basin taps were full on and the plug was in. A bubbly pink waterfall was pouring all over the floor.

Toby had discovered Jessica's bubble bath. Max squelched across the room and turned the taps off.

"Toby!" he hissed.

There was no answer and no sign of his gargoyle friend.

"What have you been doing?" cried Mum. Max turned round. Mum and Dad were standing behind him, looking in horror at the flood.

"I didn't do it!" exclaimed Max. "I didn't even wash my hands!"

"You always try to wriggle out of it," said Dad crossly as Mum threw towels down to soak up the water. "I've had enough of your pranks, Max. Go to your room. No more apple crumble and no TV tonight."

Max thought about it. He was sorry not to be finishing his pudding but he had a much more important mission: Find Toby. Who knew what other mischief the gargoyle was going to get up to?

He rushed into his bedroom. He looked under his bed and in his cupboard and rummaged through the pile of underpants. No gargoylz.

"Time to find clues, Agent Black," he said to himself.

He went back to the bathroom, tiptoeing in case his parents heard. No Toby there. But on the landing carpet he saw a line of small bubbly pawprints. "Excellent," he muttered. "I have a lead." The prints trailed across to Jessica's room. He leaned over the banister and listened. His family

was still eating crumble.
The coast was clear.
He followed the prints.

"Greetingz!" An upside-
down monkey face flashed
backwards and forwards
in front of him. Toby was
swinging from Jessica's
frilly lampshade. Max
looked around in
dismay. Jessica's toy box had
been emptied, every drawer was open
and there was green playdough covered in
tooth marks all over the floor.

"Did you make this mess?" Max
demanded, zooming round
putting everything back to
rights. He couldn't believe
he was tidying his sister's
bedroom!

"I was looking for more
biscuits," Toby explained.

194

"But all I found was that horrible green stuff. **Bleurgh!** Tasted disgusting."

"Come back to my room before you get me into worse trouble." Max went to the door to make sure there was no one about.

"Dangling drainpipes!" said Toby as he flew along the landing. "I haven't had this much fun since I put sneezing powder in the vicar's hankie! Let's play a trick on your family."

"I wish we could," sighed Max. "But I'd end up with no pudding for a week. I'd never survive. You'll have to try and behave yourself till tomorrow."

Back in his bedroom, Max rummaged under his pillow and found his Game Boy. "I've got this really cool game," he told Toby. "It's called Attack of the Martian Mushrooms. I'll play it first to show you what to do and then you can have a go." He showed Toby the brightly flashing screen. "You can hold it in your paws, can't you?"

"Course I can," said Toby, squatting down to watch.

Max clicked some buttons and started the game. He escaped in a rocket before the mushrooms captured him. Then, with some amazing skill, he leaped to level sixty-two. "One more minute and you can have a go, Toby," he murmured as he concentrated on blasting the Monster Fungus that had him in its evil tendrils.

At last he had reached the Toadstool of Terror. "I'll just save my game and—" Max suddenly realized it had gone very quiet in his bedroom. He looked up. Toby was nowhere to be seen.

"Oh, no," he groaned, leaping to his feet. "Not again!"

He sped across the landing, checking every room. He peered inside the airing cupboard and pulled out all the clothes in the dirty washing basket, scattering them on the carpet.

No gargoyle in sight!

There was only one thing for it. Agent Black was going to have to venture into enemy territory. He would have to go downstairs and search there – and all without his parents seeing him.

"Activate invisibility shield," he muttered.

He crept down the stairs and checked the hall. The door to the cupboard under the stairs was open. He flashed past the lounge with an expert commando roll and stuck his head into the cupboard. It was a total mess. Shoes, cloths, polish – everything looked as if it had been picked up and tossed in the air.

Good, thought Max. *Toby's been here. I'm getting close*.

He shut the door so no one would notice the disaster area and moved stealthily on to the kitchen. He put his secret listening device – codename: Ear – to the door. He could hear a lot of splashing. He opened the door a crack – and gawped! Toby was sitting in the sink, playing with the pots and pans. The water was slopping over the edge and the room was filled with bubbles of washing-up liquid.

Max slid across the wet floor. He put his hands into the soapy water to grab his gargoyle friend. "Toby!" he gasped. "You've got to come—"

"What have you got there?"

Max's spy radar went into overdrive: small, shriekingly loud and a complete pest. He knew what that meant. It was Enemy Agent Jessica Black, codename: Disgusting Little Sister. She was pointing at Toby, who was sitting in a saucepan.

"It's nothing," Max said quickly, moving to stand in between his sister and the soapy gargoyle.

"You've got an animal there," she insisted, trying to push past him. "Let me see it."

"No, Jess," said Max through gritted teeth. "Go away!"

"Mum!" yelled Jessica.

"Be quiet," begged Max. "I'll give you anything you want, only don't get Mum in here."

"MUM!" Jessica stuck her tongue out at him and ran to the door. "MUM!" she bellowed down the hall. "Max has come downstairs. He's playing in the kitchen with a monkey."

"Quick, Toby," hissed Max. "You have to hide!" He looked frantically round the room. There was only one place he could think of. "Can you hold your breath?"

"Yes." Toby grinned. "For ages!" He closed his mouth and ducked under the bubbles just as Mum burst into the kitchen. Jessica peered slyly round her from the hall.

"What are you doing, Max?" demanded his mother. She looked very angry. "You were told to stay in your bedroom."

Agent Max had to put his super brain into gear and think fast. "I was . . ." he began. Then it came to him. "I felt so bad

200

about the mess I made upstairs that I came down to do the washing up for you," he declared triumphantly, splashing his hands about in the water and pulling out a wooden spoon.

"Oh, Max," said his mum, her face softening. "That's so sweet. Thank you. We'll leave you to it." She turned to Jessica. "Come on, Jess," she said brightly. "Bedtime."

"But I want to see the monkey!" Jessica wailed.

"What monkey?" asked Mum.

"Max has got a monkey in the sink."

Max didn't know how long Toby could hold his breath. He had to get rid of Mum and Jessica quickly. More fast thinking was needed. He picked up the sponge and squeezed it so it looked like a mouth.

"Ooo-ooo, eee-eee!" he squeaked, making the sponge jiggle about. "This is what she thought was a monkey. I was just mucking about."

"**NOOOOO!**" yelled Jessica, stamping her foot. "He had a real monkey. It had ears and a tail."

Mum peered at the soapy suds. Then she grabbed Jessica and hauled her out of the door.

"Nice story, Jess," she said, "but you have to go to bed now."

They went, Jessica protesting all the way.

With a huge splutter, Toby burst out of the water.

"That was close," breathed Max. He looked at all the dirty plates. "But now we've got to do the washing up for real."

"Dangling drainpipes!" exclaimed Toby. "Can't wait. I love water and bubblz."

He stuck the sponge on his arrow-shaped tail, grabbed a plate in each front paw and scrubbed them clean.

"Awesome!" cried Max. "Two in one go. Wish I had a tail."

They soon had everything washed and piled in a wobbly tower on the draining board.

"Great work!" said Max, impressed. "And we only broke a plate and three glasses."

There was a noise from the hall. Toby jumped into the breadbin as Dad came in.

"Good job, Max." He patted him on the shoulder. "Go off and play now. I'll do the drying up."

"Thanks, Dad," said Max. He sidled round towards where Toby was hidden. Somehow he had to get him out of the room without Dad seeing. He opened the breadbin a crack. There was Toby, tucking into a large crusty loaf.

"You can't do that!" Max whispered. "That's breakfast."

"Max, why are you talking to the

breadbin?" Dad asked, puzzled.

"I saw a mouse in there," said Max. He made a grab for Toby and stuffed him up his jumper. "It's OK. I've got it. I'll take it away."

He slipped out of the kitchen and dashed up to his bedroom, leaving Dad staring at the bread and the large, gargoyle-shaped teeth marks in it.

"Right!" Max said, shaking Toby out onto the bed and snatching up his Game Boy. "It's your turn now."

Toby gave a huge yawn. "Too tired," he said in a sleepy voice. "Bedtime."

He scrambled up into the wardrobe and made himself comfortable,

hanging upside-down from a coat hanger.
Soon Max could hear rumbling snores.

That'll keep him out of trouble, he thought
in relief, *until I get him back to school in the
morning. Then he can play all the tricks he
wants!*

4. Science and Snakes

Brrrrrrring! The bell rang for the end of school. Everyone in Year Four jostled out of Oldacre Primary and rushed home. Everyone except Max and Ben. They were mooching along the corridor to Science Club.

"It's not fair!" moaned Max, dragging his feet. "Why should Miss Bleet force us to go to a stupid club after school? It's taking up valuable gargoyle time. We haven't seen Toby and his friends all day."

"It's not like we did anything wrong," agreed Ben. "We only put sherbet in Miss

Bleet's coffee to see what would happen. It bubbled up really nicely. I'd have thought that was enough science for one week."

Max opened the classroom door. His spy radar immediately picked up on someone in the front row: skinny, knobbly knees, ponytail. Max knew what that meant. It was Enemy Agent Lucinda Tellingly, codename: Bossy Boots. She was sitting smugly with her friend Tiffany. She stuck her tongue out at him. "I thought things couldn't get any worse," he muttered.

He and Ben sidled in to take their places at the back of the classroom and Max's spy radar whirred into action again: tall, bald, glasses on the end of his nose. It was Enemy Agent Mr Widget, codename: Boffin.

SPY FILE:

Codename: Boffin

Mr Widget gulped as he saw them arrive. "Now we're all here at last," he said, rubbing his hands together nervously. "We're going to have such a good time!"

"I bet!" groaned Max under his breath.

"We are going outside to collect worms for a new wormery," Mr Widget continued.

Max let out a deafening whoop of joy and did a high-five with Ben. Maybe Science Club wouldn't be so bad after all.

"Glad you're so keen, boys." Mr Widget beamed, wiping his forehead with relief. "Now get into pairs, take one of these buckets of soapy water each – and follow me."

"Yuck!" came a disgusted muttering from Lucinda. "Why can't we pick flowers like we did last week?"

The Science Club kids marched out of school and over to the sports field, which was hidden behind a row of trees. They tried not to spill the contents of their red plastic buckets on the way.

"I wonder what this is for," said Max as he and Ben slopped along, leaving a trail of soapy water behind them. "Worms don't need washing, do they?"

Science Club arrived at the field. The far end was covered in sports equipment. The whole school had been practising for Sports Day. There were boxes of beanbags and balls, hoops and sacks.

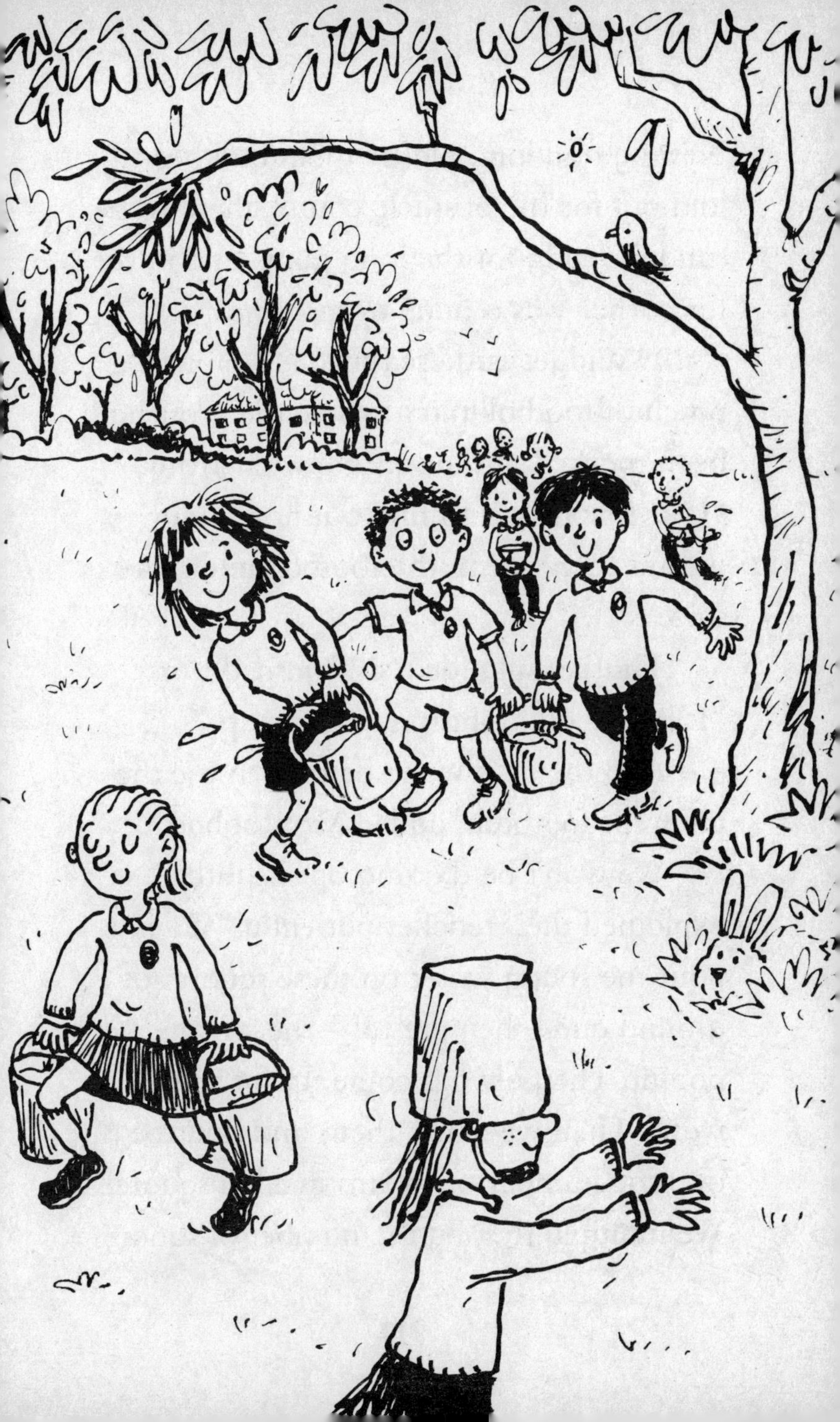

Netting and long plastic tubes had been laid out for the obstacle course, there was a sandpit ready for the long jump, and in the far corner was a huge trampoline.

Mr Widget gathered the club around a patch of football pitch where the grass had been marked out in squares with string. "Our first task is to find out how many worms there are in the football pitch," he said.

"That's a silly idea, sir!" gasped Ben. "It'll take all night to dig them up."

"And then we won't be able to use the pitch for football," added Max, aghast.

"We won't be digging up the pitch," explained their teacher patiently. "We just pour the soapy water on these squares of ground and – hey presto! – the worms pop up. They always come up for soapy water. Then we count them and find the average number of worms in each square. We multiply that by the number of squares

that are marked out which gives us the number of worms in a quarter of the pitch, then we multiply that by four and – hey presto! – we find out how many worms there are in the whole pitch. Couldn't be simpler."

"Don't know what he's going on about," said Max, chucking some water on their patch. "Let's just find those worms!"

"Do we have to say *hey presto!* sir?" asked Ben.

"That will not be necessary," sighed Mr Widget. "When you have finished counting, you may each catch one worm and place it carefully in this pot of earth I've brought along. These will be the

worms for the new wormery."

All the kids in Science Club poured
the water over their squares of grass and
eagerly knelt down to wait. Max and Ben
stared at their bubbly patch of earth. At
first nothing happened. Then suddenly
a little pink worm popped up behind a
dandelion. There were squeals of horror
from Lucinda and Tiffany as worms
appeared on their patch of grass as well.

"Cool!" exclaimed Ben, watching all
the worms wriggle to the surface. "It's
working. Let's put some more water down
and see if we can break the World Record
for Worms in a Square." He turned to
pick up the bucket, but it wasn't there.

"Someone's taken our water!" he declared indignantly.

The boys looked round. Max could just make out something red and plastic hidden in the hedge. "It's over there."

They hurried over. Sure enough, the bucket was hidden amongst the thickest leaves.

"How did it get in here?" Ben wondered.

"Afternoon," said a gurgly voice and a grumpy stone face appeared from behind the bucket.

"It's Bart!" cried Ben in delight as the round-bellied gargoyle waddled out.

"Have you come to join Science Club?" asked Max. "It's great. It's all about worms."

"Certainly not!" declared Bart grouchily. "Trying to get rid of Science Club."

Theo's cat-like head appeared from

the other side of the bucket. "We want
to get our pawz on the sports things,"
he explained, pointing a claw at the
equipment at the other end of the field.

"Been looking at it all day from the
church tower," grumbled Bart. "Thought
now school's finished we'd get our chance.
Then Science Club came out."

"I can't wait to play with the balls," said
Theo.

POP! Zack appeared out of thin air.
"Beanbagz and bats! Beanbagz and bats!"
he chanted, jumping up and down and
shaking the whole hedge.

"I wanted to explore those tubez" said a
shy voice.

Max peered deeper into the hedge. Barney was hiding there, the spikes on his back quivering with excitement.

"But why did you take our bucket?" asked Ben.

"If we collect all the buckets," said Bart, "Science Club won't be able to do any more science. Everyone will go away and leave us alone."

"Toby's doing it," added Barney. "It should have been Zack because he can make himself invisible but he kept reappearing by accident. He was nearly seen by the humanz."

There was a wheezy panting noise behind them and the boys turned to see Toby trying to haul a heavy bucket across the grass, water slopping everywhere. He wasn't getting

very far. Suddenly he spotted the boys. He let go and flew back to the hedge.

"Greetingz." He grinned. "You're here just at the right time. I need you to collect all the buckets."

"It won't work," Max told him. "Everyone will just come looking for them like we did. You'll be keeping them here, not driving them away."

Toby scratched his stone chin. "Hmm," he said. "You may be right." He turned to his friends. "Listen, gargoylz, Trick One isn't working. We need Trick Two."

"What's Trick Two?" asked Max. "Can we help? Finding worms was fun but counting them will be boring."

"Max and Ben," came their teacher's voice. "What are you doing?"

Mr Widget was staring at them suspiciously.

"Er . . . some buckets rolled away, sir," called Ben. "We're just getting them back."

"Got to go," Max whispered to the gargoylz. "We don't want Mr Widget coming over here and finding you."

The boys grabbed the buckets and ran back to their square of ground. Suddenly a terrible stink filled the air and a wheezy laugh could be heard from the hedge.

"I think we've found out what Trick Two was." Ben grinned as the kids yelled in horror and dashed for the gate.

"Barney's made one of his special pongs! I hope the gargoylz have a good time on the sports stuff."

The boys held their noses and slowly walked after the rest of the fleeing Science Club. But the terrible smell didn't last long. Mr Widget headed the kids off at the gate and herded them all back to their task.

"Can't be put off by a silly little smell!" he exclaimed, picking up his pot. "Now start counting. And I'll come and collect your chosen worms."

"He's too busy to notice us for a moment," whispered Max. "And counting's boring. Let's go and find out if there's a Trick Three."

The two boys crept back to the hedge where the gargoylz were gathered in a circle, muttering to each other. Just then a stone head emerged from the leaves. It was a gargoyle that the boys hadn't seen before. It had plump cheeks and a wide grinning mouth, but instead of hair, stone snakes wriggled all round its head. The snakes writhed as if they were fighting.

"Wow!" breathed Max. "Who are you?"

"This is Eli," explained Toby. "Say hello to Max and Ben, Eli."

Eli looked horrified – and his snakes stood on end in shock. "Humanssssss!" he hissed.

"These are our friends," said Toby patiently. "They play tricks like us."

Eli's look of horror turned to a slow smile and the snakes on his head bobbed merrily at the boys.

"Eli is Trick Three," Toby went on. "He's going to use his special power to scare everyone off the field. Ready, Eli?"

To the boys' surprise, the snaky gargoyle suddenly vanished.

"Where's he gone?" asked Max, puzzled. "Can he make himself invisible like Zack?"

"Not exactly invisible . . ." said Toby mysteriously.

The next minute there was a yell from one of the kids counting worms.

"I've found a snake, sir!"

Toby grinned. "That's Eli," he said proudly. "He can turn into a snake."

They watched as Mr Widget rushed over to take a look, with the rest of Science Club following curiously behind him. Even Lucinda and Tiffany were edging cautiously forwards.

Toby gave a growly chuckle. "This is going to be more fun than the time I put earwigz in the vicar's wellies. Any minute

now all those humanz will be screaming
and running for their lives and we can
have the sports things to ourselves!"

There was a muffled "Hurray!" from the
hedge, and several pairs of eager stone eyes
peeped through the leaves.

Mr Widget was now peering down at
Eli. He still clutched his pot of worms. "A
grass snake!" he exclaimed enthusiastically.
"How interesting – and quite harmless.
Look at its black spots and yellow collar."
The children all jostled to look.

"No one's run away yet," commented
Barney.

"I knew that idea wouldn't work,"
said Bart gloomily. "Kids aren't scared of
snakes. At least not grass snakes, and that's
all Eli can do."

"What about Trick Four?" asked Theo, swishing his tail.

"Haven't got a Trick Four," said Toby with a frown.

The gargoylz all looked despondent.

"I have!" exclaimed Max. "Lucinda and Tiffany are getting very twitchy about the worms and the snake has nearly finished them off. What if Zack makes himself invisible so no one will see him? Then he creeps up behind Mr Widget and knocks the worm pot out of his hand. Ben and I can make sure the worms land on Lucinda and Tiffany. People will hear their screams all the way to the moon!"

"Good one, Agent Black," said Ben. "Mr Widget will have to take them back to school and that will be the end of Science Club for today."

"Brilliant!" cried Zack, racing round in excited circles. Max noticed with relief that everyone in Science Club was still staring at Eli, so nobody spotted Zack. "Let's go!"

"Not yet, Zack," called Ben. "We've got to get everyone in position."

But it was too late. **POP!** Zack had vanished.

"Run!" Max told Ben urgently. "We've got to be there when the worms are spilled."

Max and Ben charged over to Mr Widget and stood just behind him, pretending to be keen to see the snake.

"He does look real," Max whispered as they watched Eli slither about the grass, his forked tongue darting in and out.

"Grass snakes should not be confused with adders," Mr Widget was telling his audience. "Adders are poisonous and— **Ooof!**"

He stumbled forward as if he had been given a hard push. Max caught a glimpse of Zack's dragony tail as it became visible for a second.

"Let me help you, sir," shouted Ben, making a grab for the pot. He gave it a quick upward jolt and the worms were flung in the air – falling all over Lucinda and Tiffany.

"Hurra— I mean, oh dear!" exclaimed Max, trying to hide his glee as the two terrified girls shrieked and jumped in shock, knocking buckets of soapy water over everyone's feet. Groans and complaints filled the air.

"I'm so sorry," said Ben, putting on his wide-eyed innocent look. "Let me help." Trying not to laugh, he started to pick worms out of Lucinda's hair. "Ooops! So sorry. That one went down your back."

"**AAAARRRGGHH!**" Lucinda screamed and sprinted for the gates, Tiffany close behind her.

"Wait!" blustered Mr Widget. "Or rather – yes, right, let's go in, everybody. Quickly now. All together. We'll collect worms another day."

Max and Ben followed the others out of the field, then Mr Widget locked the gates. Max and Ben peered back through the bars.

The gargoylz were having the time of their lives. Zack was darting about throwing beanbags to Theo, Barney's spikes were just disappearing down one of the tubes and Bart was playing in the sandpit. Eli was back to his normal self, bouncing on the trampoline, his snaky hair jiggling.

"Where's Toby?" whispered Max.

"Here I am," came a growly purr and

Toby flew up to perch on the gates. He was grinning broadly. "Thanks, Max and Ben," he said. "Now we're going to have the best gargoyle sports day ever!"

Book Three:
Gargoylz at a Midnight Feast

1. Sports Day Mischief

Max Black and his best friend, Ben Neal, nine-year-old super secret agents, were on their way to school. They had an important mission.

"Ready for action, Agent Neal?" asked Max.

Ben nodded. "Ready, Agent Black."

Max bent down and tied his right leg tightly to Ben's left with his school scarf. He straightened up. "We're sure to win the three-legged race at Sports Day after all this practice. Go!"

The boys lurched forwards, wobbled

and fell over.

"Better sort out our technique if we're going to break the world record," said Ben, rubbing his knee.

"Let's try again," said Max as they staggered to their feet. "The starter has raised his pistol . . . wait for it . . . **BANG**!"

They bounded off down the road, this time without a stumble.

Max's spy radar picked up someone in the distance: pale, skinny, frilly socks. He knew what that meant. It was Enemy Agent Lucinda Tellingly, codename: Bossy Boots.

They whizzed past her, making her ponytail fly.

"You don't stand a chance!" she called after them nastily.

Ben twisted round to stick his tongue out and fell into a hedge, taking Max with him. Lucinda cackled loudly.

"She'll be sorry when we beat her and the rest of Year Four," said Max, pulling leaves out of his spiky dark hair.

They untangled themselves and belted off again at breakneck speed.

"Awesome pace!" panted Ben. "I can't

wait for this afternoon. Sports Day's the best day of the school year, apart from Christmas Dinner Day."

"Every school day's cool now we've got our secret friends," said Max.

They reached the gates of Oldacre Primary and flung their arms round the gatepost to stop. Max peered up at the ancient church next door. The gutters and spouts were decorated with carved gargoylz. Only Max and Ben knew that the little stone creatures were alive and loved to play tricks – just like the boys.

They made for the wall between the playground and the church.

"Greetingz," came a growly purr.

A gargoyle with a monkey face, big pointy ears and sparkling eyes was sitting on a gravestone in the churchyard. It was Toby.

"Dangling drainpipes!" he exclaimed. "Two headz? Three legz? Have you turned

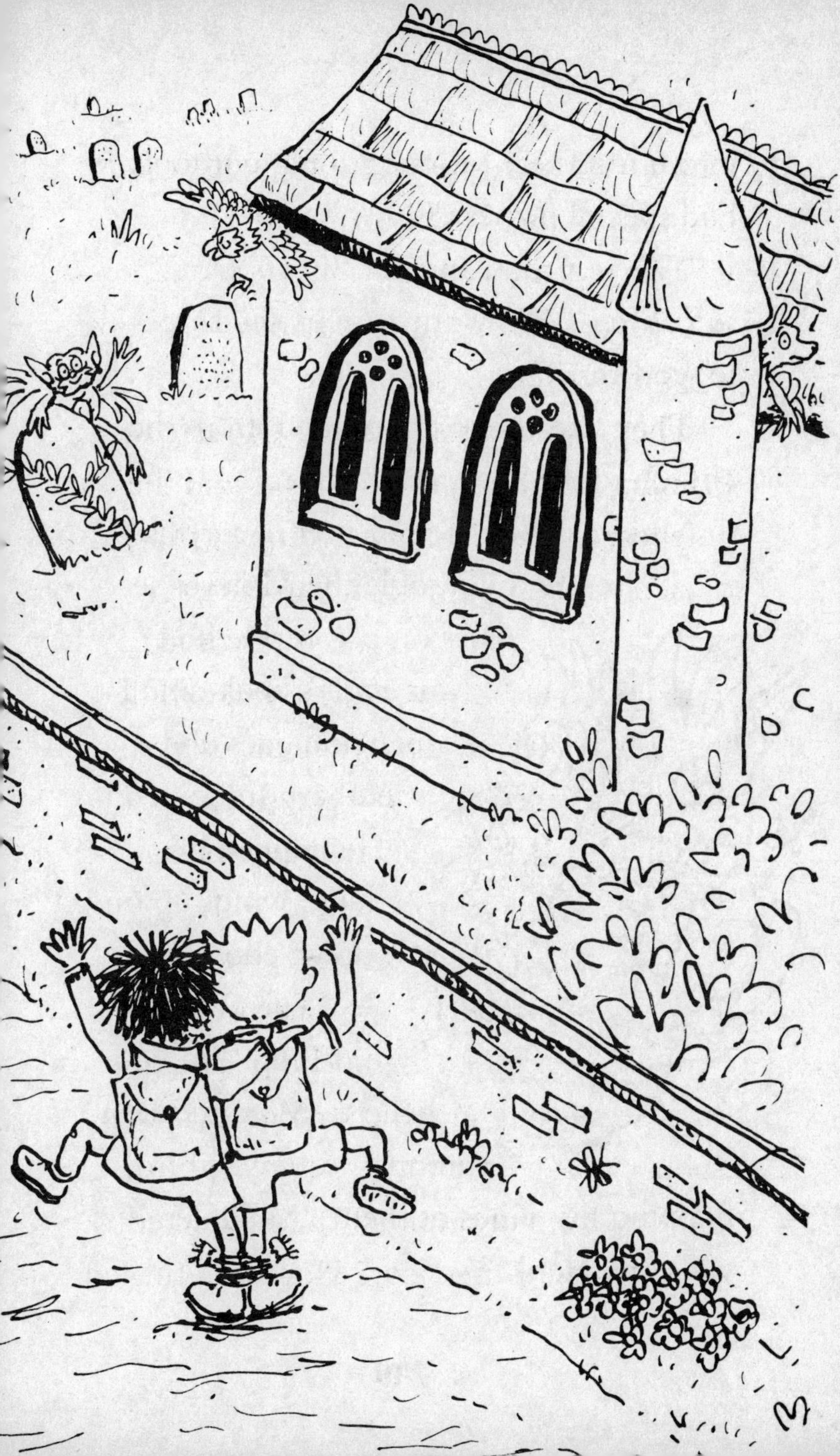

into a monster? I thought only gargoylz had special powerz."

"We're practising for Sports Day," said Max. "We want to win the three-legged race."

They heard a sharp squawk from the church roof. "Shiver me timbers!"

Max and Ben looked over in surprise to see a gargoyle they'd never set eyes on before. He had an eagle's beak, small piercing eyes and a feathery stone head. He flapped his large wings up and down eagerly.

"This is Ira," said Toby. "Ira, say hello to Max and Ben."

"Humanz!" squawked Ira, flapping his wings at them. "Make 'em walk the plank!"

"I've told you about Max and Ben,"
said Toby patiently. "They're our friendz."

"Part of the crew?" asked Ira
suspiciously.

"Yes, they'll keep our secret," Toby
assured him. "They're almost as good
as gargoylz."

"Welcome aboard then," said Ira,
saluting with a wing.

"Why does he talk like that?" Ben
whispered to Toby.

"He's never been the same since a parrot from a pirate ship landed on him," explained Toby. "Now he thinks he's a pirate too."

"Outrageous!" came a shriek from across the playground.

Toby and Ira froze.

Max's radar burst into action: grey hair, beaky nose, evil eyes flashing. He knew what that meant. It was Enemy Agent Mrs Hogsbottom, commonly known as Mrs Hogsbum, codename: Evil Head Teacher.

Mrs Hogsbottom strode up to them, making the playground shake. "How dare you break school rule number eight hundred and forty-three: boys must not use their stripy school scarves to tie their legs together!"

"We're practising for the three-legged race this afternoon," Ben tried to explain.

"We want to break the world record," added Max.

"No excuses!" snapped Mrs Hogsbottom. She marched off and shouted at some girls who were singing too happily.

The gargoylz unfroze.

"Nasty old landlubber!" squawked Ira.

"I'd love to see you break the world record," said Toby wistfully.

"Why don't you come and watch?" suggested Max.

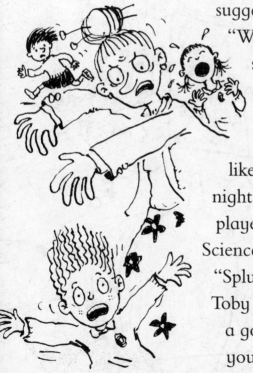

"We'll be on the school field all afternoon. You can hide in the hedge like you did last night when we played that trick on Science Club."

"Spluttering gutterz!" Toby grinned. "What a good idea. See you there."

I t was a bright, sunny afternoon and
Sports Day started right after lunch.
Everything was ready.

When no one was looking, Max and Ben sidled over to the hedge and peered through the leaves. Seven pairs of stone eyes stared back at them.

"You've all come to watch," said Max. "Awesome!"

A dog-faced gargoyle with spines down his back smiled at them shyly. "Toby says you're going to break the world record."

"Too right, Barney," Ben told him. He looked over at the board of events. "Our race is last," he groaned. "That's ages."

"Time for a trick then," said Max.

The gargoylz gave a great cheer.

Max whipped a small pot out of his
pocket. "This is the perfect way to get
Lucinda back for being mean to us on the
way to school. She's in the sack race next,
with all her friends. Time for Secret Plan:
Itchy Surprise."

Ben read the label aloud: "*Jimmy Joker's
Best Itching Powder*. Just the
thing, Agent Black. I can't
wait to see Lucinda's face
when she starts scratching.
But how do we put it in the
sacks without being seen?"

"Ssspluttering guttersss!
That sounds like a trick for me
to play." A gargoyle with a head covered
with wriggling snakes grinned up at him.

"Brilliant plan, Eli," said Max, handing
the pot to him. "Off you go."

Eli took the pot in his mouth, turned
into a grass snake and slithered off towards
the pile of brown sacks. He was soon back

Lucinda and the other racers climbed into their sacks and stood eagerly at the starting line.

"*I* haven't bothered to practise," Lucinda said loudly, seeing Max and Ben watching. "I'll win anyway."

"Ready, steady, **wheeeee**!" Mr Widget blew the starting whistle. The race began. The competitors bounced along the grass,

cheered on by their classmates. But one
by one they began to jump about wildly,
scratching all over. Max and Ben found it
hard to keep a straight face when Lucinda
shot out of her sack and ran off, shrieking.
Finally Mr Widget called the race off.

"OUTRAGEOUS!" bellowed Mrs Hogsbottom from her special head teacher's chair. "Give them all extra homework!"

There was a volley of gargoyle cackles from the hedge.

"Exsssellent!" declared Eli, the snakes on his head hissing in delight. "What a prank!"

"We haven't finished yet." Max grinned. "I've thought of a brilliant way to make our race come sooner. We'll speed up all the other races. What's next?"

"Infants' egg and spoon," Ben read from the board.

"Time for Secret Plan: Sticky Egg and Spoon Race," declared Max. He pulled a tube of glue from his pocket. "Follow me, Agent Neal. No one will see. They're all watching the trampolining." They sneaked over to where the special spoons and hard-boiled eggs were waiting for the infants' race.

"We'll stick every egg to a spoon," chuckled Max. "The infants won't have to wobble along for hours trying to balance them. It'll be the fastest egg and spoon race on the planet."

"Awesome plan, Agent Black," said Ben.

Max had just blobbed a drop of glue onto the first spoon when he heard a bellow. It was Mrs Hogsbottom.

"What do you think you're doing?"

"We're helping the little ones out," said Ben. "Making the race a bit easier for them." He put on his best innocent look. It always worked on the dinner ladies, who cooed over his blond hair and blue eyes and gave him extra baked beans. It never worked on Mrs Hogsbottom.

"Outrageous!" she growled, taking the glue and putting it in her pocket. "Trying to help someone cheat, were you?"

"Oh no," protested Max. "We were going to glue all of them the same."

Mrs Hogsbottom marched them over to their class. "Sit down quietly and wait for your race. And no more nonsense."

"*Nonsense?*" said Max indignantly when she'd stomped back to her chair. "We were being helpful. She could at least have said thank you."

"No chance," said Ben. "It's probably against one of her school rules." He looked over to where the obstacle race was just finishing. "It's our turn soon," he said excitedly. "Let's practise."

They charged along to their teacher, Miss Bleet.

"Can we have our leg tie, please, miss?" asked Ben. "We're running together."

"I can't possibly let you do that!" she said nervously. "You'll do something silly. I've not forgotten last year when you put flour bombs in the long jump sand."

"But we have to run together," pleaded Max. "We're going to break the world record."

"The world record will have to wait," insisted Miss Bleet. "I have a better idea. Something that will keep  you out of trouble. Ben, you'll be Tiffany's partner, and Max, you go with Lucinda."

Max and Ben gawped at their teacher.

"You can't mean—" spluttered Max.

"Tied to girls!" groaned Ben. "And not just *any* girls – Lucinda and Tiffany are the most goody-goody girls in the history of goody-goody girls!"

"They smell all flowery, miss," Max told her earnestly. "We'll die from the pong and it'll be your fault."

Miss Bleet waved him away.

Max's face suddenly lit up.

"It's Friday," he hissed happily in Ben's ear. "And it's nearly three o'clock."

Ben stared at him. "How's that going to stop us being trapped with the ghastly girls?"

Max beamed. "My sister goes to gym at the sports centre on Fridays after school. I had to promise to be ready at three so that Mum could pick us both up and get Jessica there in time." He peered at the crowd of spectators to find his mum. "She'll be waving at me any minute to say it's time to go. We're saved."

"You're forgetting one thing," said Ben miserably. "*You* might be saved but I'm not. I'm going to be tied to Tiffany Goodchild. My life is over."

"I'd forgotten that." Max frowned. "We need a special plan for you."

"Got it!" said Ben. "I'll tell Miss Bleet I've broken my leg. I can't race then."

"Excellent plan, Agent Neal," said Max. "I'll let Mum know I'm ready to go while you break the news to Miss Bleet."

Ben ran off.

"Don't forget to limp!" Max yelled after him.

Three minutes later Ben was back. Max was sitting by the hedge, his head in his hands.

"I can't believe my idea didn't work!" he groaned. "Nan's taking Jessica to gym so that Mum can watch us break the world record."

"And Miss Bleet didn't believe I'd broken my leg," said Ben sadly. "Even when I collapsed in front of her and rolled about like a footballer. Now we're doomed to be tied to those smelly girls."

"What's wrong?" said a gurgly voice. Toby popped up between them.

They told him all about the terrible fate that awaited them.

Toby smiled. "Perhaps

we could help. There must be one of our special powerz that will work."

"Awesome," said Max, cheering up. "But which one?"

Toby scratched his stony chin. "My flying won't be much use."

"And Barney's stinky smells don't work on people outdoors unless they're really close to him," said Ben.

Toby's golden eyes suddenly lit up. "We need Zack!" he declared. "Zack can make himself invisible and steal those red things Miss Bleet is going to tie your legs with."

"Perfect!" exclaimed Max. "No ties, no race. But where *is* Zack?"

POP! Zack appeared out of nowhere. He ran up and down the grass, tail swishing eagerly. "Did someone call?" he panted.

Max quickly explained what they wanted him to do. **POP!** Zack vanished. In an instant he was back, some red ties in his mouth and some draped over his fuzzy mane. Ben shoved them under the hedge and covered them with leaves.

"Take your places for the three-legged race," trumpeted Mrs Hogsbottom.

"Let's go." Max grinned. "We'd better look keen."

Miss Bleet tripped off to find the ties and the boys ran over to stand next to their partners. Lucinda scowled at Max.

Max smiled sweetly back. Any minute now their teacher would find there weren't any ties and the race would be abandoned.

But now Miss Bleet was approaching – holding some ropes. The boys gawped at her in horror.

"Couldn't find the ties," she twittered nervously. "But these will do just as well."

"Help!" Max groaned as she tied him to his partner. "I'll catch the Lucinda Lurgy being this close!"

"Shut up, horrible boy!" snapped Lucinda.

Ben tried to twist himself free from Tiffany. "I'm being overcome by dangerous girly fumes!" he gasped.

But it was too late. Mr Widget was

starting the race. "Ready . . . steady . . ."

Suddenly the sky went dark and huge drops of rain began to fall, faster and faster.

In seconds everyone was soaked to the skin.

"Outrageous!" bellowed Mrs Hogsbottom, putting up a huge black umbrella and not letting anyone share it. "School rule number four hundred and thirteen – it must *not* rain on Sports Day! Everybody inside. At the double!"

Lucinda gave a loud shriek and turned to run back into school with everyone else. But she'd forgotten she was still tied to Max. She took one step and fell face down in a puddle.

Trying not to laugh too loudly, Max and Ben hurried to undo their ropes and help Lucinda up. By the time they'd hauled her to her feet she was covered from head to foot in cold wet mud.

"Shame," giggled Ben as they watched her squelching across the grass with Tiffany. "Not our fault if a bit of extra mud accidentally got wiped all over her."

Max spotted Toby beckoning from the hedge and ran over through the teeming rain. Ben followed him across the grass. The gargoylz had big grins on their stone faces. Zack was rolling over and over, giggling helplessly.

Toby gave them a thumbs-up. "Good trick on Lucinda," he chortled. "I haven't laughed so much since we put the vicar's Harvest Festival display on the roof."

"And that rain came just at the right moment," said Max. "What luck!"

"That wasn't luck," said Toby. "That was Ira's special power."

"Ira can make it rain?" gasped Ben in amazement. "Awesome!"

"Only in short bursts," explained Toby.

"But for long enough to save us," said Max. "Thanks, Ira."

"Anything for a shipmate!" squawked Ira, saluting them from the hedge.

The rain stopped as suddenly as it had started. Ben wrung out his T-shirt. "We'd better go back to school," he said.

"See you again soon, gargoylz," Max called into the hedge. "This has been the best Sports Day ever!"

2. Barney Cooks Up a Storm

Max and Ben whirred through the
school gates in their imaginary spy
helicopter.

"Secret Mission: Spot the Gargoylz!"
whispered Max, chugging to a halt.

"Right away, Agent Black." Ben put his
hands up to his eyes like binoculars and
scanned the church roof. "No sign of them.
Not even a tail."

"Try the churchyard," suggested Max.

The boys zoomed across to the wall
between Oldacre School and the church
next door. They peered over. Five stony

shapes were huddled together in the long grass.

Max's spy radar whirred into action: small, cheeky, full of tricks. He knew what that meant. It was their secret friends, the gargoylz.

Toby's head popped up from the huddle. "Greetingz!" he called across in a doleful voice. He flew onto the wall next to the boys. Barney, Theo, Eli and Zack scrambled up to join him. The five gargoylz sat in a row, their tails drooping.

"What's wrong?" asked Max, looking at their mournful faces. "You haven't run out of pranks, have you?"

Toby shook his head. "Of course not!" he exclaimed. "That could never happen. We're just worried about Bart. You know he's always a bit grumpy . . ."

"Well, lately he's got worse . . ." Theo told the boys, his tiger ears flopping sadly.

"And now he's really misssserable," hissed Eli.

"We're trying to find a way to stop him being so down in the dumps," said Barney.

"Bounce on him?" suggested Zack, jumping up and down on his big floppy feet.

"That would probably make him grumpier than ever," laughed Max. "But there must be something we can do."

"I've got an idea!" Ben said suddenly. "Max is coming for a sleepover on

Friday night. Why don't you all come too? If you bring Bart we could give him a surprise party!"

The gargoylz looked puzzled.

"What's a sleepover?" asked Toby, scratching his stony head with one claw.

"It's when you sleep at a friend's house," explained Max. "Only you don't sleep much — you stay up really late and have a midnight feast and play games and tell stories! It's awesome!"

Toby's golden eyes lit up. "Dangling drainpipes!" he shouted. "That'll be just the thing for Bart!"

The spikes on Barney's back quivered happily and Zack jumped over Theo's head in excitement. Suddenly they all heard menacing footsteps clomping across the playground towards them. The gargoylz froze into statues.

Max activated his spy radar: grey hair, beaky nose, teeth like a crocodile. It was Enemy Agent Mrs Hogsbottom, commonly known as Mrs Hogsbum, codename: Evil Head Teacher. She had come halfway across the playground and now stopped to shout at the boys.

The gargoylz sat on the wall with frozen grins.

"School rule number three hundred and fifty-nine," yelled Mrs Hogsbottom, "boys must not put ugly stone things on school walls. Get rid of them and go to your classroom. Immediately!" She stomped off again towards her office.

"Who's she calling ugly?" protested Toby. "Her face could crack mirrors!"

"I don't think she's ever looked in a mirror," said Ben. "She'd frighten herself to death."

Max heard Mrs Hogsbum's office window opening. "Better go," he hissed. "See you later."

The boys sped off into school. When Max turned at the door and looked back, the gargoylz had gone.

"Miss Bleet's in the worst mood in the history of worst moods," muttered Max as he and Ben sat in class after play, chewing their pencils.

"Too right," agreed Ben. "Every time I read my comic instead of my English book she tells me off! Weird!"

"And when we were looking out of the window at Barney earlier she got really cross," said Max. "We told her it was important but she wouldn't listen."

"I wonder what Barney was doing running across the playground anyway," said Ben. "He had a piece of paper in his paw."

"It must have been important," said Max. "He was in such a hurry."

"Max and Ben," quavered Miss Bleet, "please stop chattering! I am having a very bad morning and you're making it worse!" She dabbed at her forehead with her hankie.

"What's wrong, miss?" asked Ben.

"There was no sugar for my coffee," she told them grumpily. "None! It's disappeared. I can't get through the morning without coffee and I can't drink coffee without sugar – especially with you two in the class!"

"I've had something
go missing too,"
piped up Tiffany.
"My chocolate bar
wasn't in my bag at
playtime."

"Nor was mine,"
called Duncan.

"And my Chocomunch
had vanished from my pocket
when I looked for it," declared Lucinda
loudly. "It was a specially big one."

Several other voices joined in until there
was a clamour of complaints around the
classroom.

"That's enough!" exclaimed Miss Bleet,
clutching her head. "You'll just have to
manage without. I'll look into it later.
Now, get on with your work."

The two boys looked at each other.

"We're the only ones who didn't have
their snacks pinched," Ben whispered to

Max. "I wonder why."

"Something very strange is going on in this school," Max whispered back. "We've got a new secret mission, Agent Neal. We must find the missing sugar and chocolate."

"Agreed, Agent Black," answered Ben. "After lunch though. It's jam sponge for pudding today. My favourite!"

"No jam sponge!" exclaimed Ben as he and Max stood at the hatch at lunch time.

"I don't believe it."

"Sorry, dear, but we couldn't make any today," Mrs Coddle the dinner lady told him. "The eggs have all disappeared. Every single one. We'll make one tomorrow. You'll have to have an apple for now." She plonked one down on Ben's plate.

Ben looked up at her with pleading blue eyes.

"Oh, you poor thing," she said, and fetched him a banana to go with it.

Max's eyes narrowed. "Our mission has changed, Agent Neal," he muttered as the boys mooched off to find a table. "There's a food thief in school – someone who likes sugar, chocolate and eggs – and it's our job to find out who it is."

As soon as they had finished their lunch, the boys ran out into the playground.

"Let's snoop around for a bit," said Max. "See if we can find a hoard of stolen food."

They sneaked about, holding imaginary magnifying glasses and trying to spot someone with a pocket full of chocolate bars.

"What's this?" Max said suddenly. There was a pile of chocolate wrappers by the staffroom window. "Is the thief one of the teachers?" He peered through the window at the teachers, who were having their lunch. No one was eating chocolate. Then a foil wrapper fluttered down from the roof. Max and Ben looked up. Barney was sitting in the gutter – covered in sticky brown goo!

"What are you up to?" asked Max curiously.

Barney went red under his goo. "I'm making chocolate chip cookiez for the midnight feast," he explained shyly. He produced a bowl and spoon and flapped

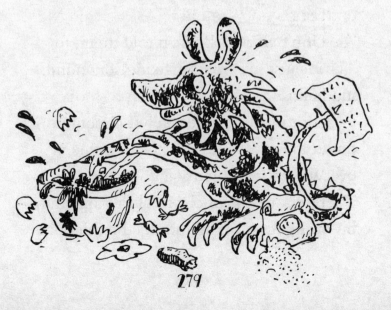

279

a piece of paper. "I got this recipe from the vicar's cookery book. Then I . . . er . . . found some sugar and eggs and chocolate." He licked his lips. "Chocolate," he sighed. "Yum!"

Max and Ben looked at each other.

"So the mystery of the food thief is solved!" Max whispered to Ben. "Great idea, Barney," he called up, "but how are you going to cook the cookies?"

There was a small roar from the roof and Max and Ben jumped in alarm as a long flame suddenly flickered over the guttering.

"Don't worry," Barney told them. "That's just my friend Azzan. Come and say hello, Azzan."

A dragon-like gargoyle with scaly skin and a long swishing tail poked his head over the edge of the roof.

"Humanz!" he cried in alarm, opening his mouth and taking a huge breath.

Barney quickly reached out a paw and clamped his jaws shut.

"No more fire, Azzan!" he said, looking worried. "These are our friends. We don't want to frazzle them."

"I'm baking the cookiez," said Azzan proudly when Barney finally let go.

"You know my special power is making smellz," Barney told the boys. "Well, Azzan's is breathing fire."

"That's great!" said Ben, wide-eyed in amazement.

"There's only one problem," Barney explained. "Azzan's fire doesn't last very long and he can't always control it – a bit like me and my smellz. Some of my cooking got a tiny bit burned." He scuttled off and came back with a tray. It was covered in smouldering black cookies.

"It's OK." Azzan grinned. "We've got plenty more ingredients. Come and look."

Max and Ben scrambled onto a nearby dustbin so that they could see onto the

roof. The dragony gargoyle was pushing
his nose into a pile of chocolate bars,
sugar and boxes of eggs. A little flame
suddenly shot out of his mouth and set
fire to one of the boxes.

"Ooops!" Azzan cried, and jumped up
and down on it. By the time the flames
had gone out he was knee-deep in egg
yolk. "Never mind," he said chirpily.
"Plenty more where they came from."

"You've got about sixty eggs there!"
exclaimed Max. "You won't need all those
for the cookies."

"Won't we?" said Barney. "Oh dear.

What shall we do with them?"

"We must give some back to the dinner ladies," said Ben, looking worried. "Otherwise they won't be able to make their yummy jam sponge tomorrow."

"Tell you what," said Max, "we'll take the eggs you don't need – that's most of them – back to the kitchen."

"But what if someone sees you?" protested Barney anxiously as he and Azzan carefully handed the boxes of eggs down to the boys. "Theo nearly got caught by a human waving a big ladle when he was getting them for me."

"Good point," said Max, scratching his head for a moment. "Got it! Azzan, we'll need your help with a trick. You just have to sneak in through that door there and breathe some flames onto the fire detector – that's the round white thing on the ceiling in the corridor. That'll make the alarm go off and everyone will think there's a fire and leave the building."

"And we'll put the eggs back while the dinner ladies are out in the playground!" finished Ben. "Brilliant idea, Agent Black!"

"A prank! A prank! We're going to do a prank!" chanted Barney. A terrible pong filled the air.

"Barney's done a bottom burp!" wheezed Azzan in delight, sending a small burst of sparks dancing across the roof.

Clutching the egg boxes, Max and Ben sneaked off behind the bins that stood next to the kitchen window. From there they watched Azzan shin down the drainpipe and slip in through the nearest door. A few seconds later – **clang! clang! clang!** – a loud alarm bell rang out across the school.

Azzan scampered back to the roof and soon everyone was pouring out of the buildings into the playground, shrieking and yelling. The dinner ladies burst out of the kitchen, carrying dishcloths and wooden spoons.

SECRET CODEWORD:
JOKE

"Go, go, go!" Agent Black cried. "The kitchen should be empty now."

The two boys slipped in through the window. Suddenly a door opened on the other side of the room. They dived down behind a counter and squeezed onto a shelf between a sausage-making machine and a giant teapot.

Max's spy radar whirred into action: stout legs, white overall, strong smell of mashed potato. He knew what that meant. It was Mrs Simmer, chief cook, codename: Manic Masher. She marched towards the boys' hiding place.

"There's a fire," they heard her mutter. "I must rescue my potato masher!"

Max and Ben held their breath as Mrs
Simmer's footsteps went past them. She
opened a drawer above their heads, took
something out and then hurried off into
the playground.

"I thought she was never going
to leave," said Ben. "I was dead
uncomfortable. I was sitting on the
teapot spout."

"She shouldn't have hung around," said
Max disapprovingly as the boys crawled
out of their hiding place. "She could've
got burned."

"It wasn't a real fire," Ben reminded him.

"Yeah, but she didn't know that," insisted Max.

Ben nodded in agreement. "Grown-ups are idiots."

They put the eggs on the counter, high-fived and raced to join their class, just as Miss Bleet was calling the register.

After school Max and Ben tore out into the playground.

"Can't wait to see how Barney's cookies are coming on," said Ben. "He should have made plenty by now."

"Hope he lets us try one," said Max. "Look, he's over there on the church roof."

They ran into the churchyard and
peered up at the porch. Barney was
clutching a large bowl and trying to stop
Toby and Azzan dipping their paws in it.
A runny brown mixture
slopped over the rim.

"Hey, Barney,"
called Max.
"How's the
cooking going?"

"Not very well,
I'm afraid," Barney
admitted sadly.
"Toby put too much
butter in one batch,
Azzan set fire to the next lot and this is my
last bowlful. I'm *not* going to let anything
happen to it."

He held it out to show the boys. As he
did, there was a **POP!** and Zack suddenly
appeared out of thin air, racing up the wall
of the church.

"Where are the cookiez?" he yelled, springing eagerly onto the porch and landing in the middle of the gargoylz. The bowl of cookie mixture was knocked clean out of Barney's paws and flew up into the air. **Splat!** It landed upside down on Barney's head, and Max and Ben and the gargoylz were all covered in sticky chocolate goo.

For a moment there was silence. Then everyone burst out laughing.

"Spluttering gutterz!" gasped Toby. "I haven't had such fun since Azzan ran along the washing line and singed the vicar's knickers!"

Barney pushed the mixing bowl off his head and it tumbled over the edge of the roof. Ben caught it.

"Don't know why I bothered trying to cook this," Barney said, licking his lips as his friends started slurping up the spilled cookie mixture. "It's delicious as it is!"

Max and Ben dipped their fingers into the bowl and tried a bit for themselves.

"You're right!" declared Max with a grin.

"It's scrumptious!" Ben agreed.

And then everyone was too busy slurping to say anything else at all.

3. Secret Plan: Free Theo

It was Friday evening. Secret Agent Max
Black sped along the pavement in his
imaginary spy motor boat with a top
secret cargo in his rucksack. He had to get
to fellow Agent Ben Neal's headquarters
without delay.

He swerved to a halt at Ben's front door.

"Can I get out now?" came a grumpy
voice from the rucksack. "That was a very
uncomfortable ride."

"Sorry, Bart," Max whispered over his
shoulder as he rang the bell. "But you'll
have to wait a bit longer. Someone might

spot you here – and you know gargoylz mustn't be seen by humans."

"Hmmph!" came the cross reply. "Where are we anyway?"

"Can't tell you," said Max. "But I think you'll like it."

Bart had been extra grumpy recently so Max, Ben and the other gargolyz had arranged a surprise sleepover to cheer him up.

The front
door opened.

"Hello, Max,"
said Ben's mum,
showing him in. "Ben's
in his room. Go on up."

Max leaped up the stairs and
knocked on Ben's bedroom door.

"Top secret delivery, Agent Neal," he
whispered.

The door opened a little and Ben's
beaming face could be seen through the
gap. "Is the coast clear, Agent Black?"
he asked.

"Clear," answered Max. Ben let him in.

Max opened his rucksack. "About time too," grumbled Bart, climbing out and straightening his gladiator's skirt. "I don't enjoy being shaken about like a—"

Bart stopped and his pointed ears shot up in amazement. He was in a bedroom, and there in front of him, in a grinning row on the bed, sat Toby, Zack, Eli and Barney.

"Sleepover surprise at Ben's house!" yelled the gargoylz.

"Spluttering gutterz!" exclaimed Bart.

"How did you all get here?"

Toby grinned, his golden eyes flashing. "I flew all the way."

"I came in Ben's rucksack after school," added Barney.

"I turned into a sssnake and ssslithered here," Eli told him. "I made the girl in next door's garden ssscream," he added. The snakes on his head giggled at this in a hissy sort of way.

"I was invisible," said Zack, bouncing on the bed and knocking the other gargoylz over. "Well – most of the time."

"Everyone's going to sleep here tonight," Ben told Bart. "We're going to have fun. Here's our midnight feast." He pulled a huge chocolate cake and a bottle of fizzy drink from under the bed.

The gargoylz sat up, tongues hanging out. "It's going to be awesome."

"Is it?" said Bart doubtfully.

"And I've brought cookies!" said Max, taking a tin out of his rucksack. "Jessica made them with Mum – and gave some to me! Can't think what came over her."

"Cookiez and cake. Cookiez and cake!" shouted Zack excitedly, bounding about the bedroom.

"Everyone's here," said Barney eagerly. "Let's start the feast now."

"Feasts are silly," said Bart.

The other gargoylz dived for the cake.

"It's not midnight yet," said Ben, sliding it quickly back under the bed.

"Besides — anyone seen Theo?" asked Max, looking around.

"That's odd," said Eli. "He ssset off when I did. He changed into a kitten first, of courssse."

"He should be here by now then," said Max, puzzled.

"I'll go down and have a look outside," suggested Ben. "He might not remember which house to come to."

"Well, he is only four hundred and twelve," said Toby. "Young gargoylz aren't very good at directions."

Ben went off downstairs. In an instant he was back, a look of horror on his face.

"Arabella's got him!" he gasped. "My stupid sister thinks he's a real cat. She's made him a bed on the windowsill with a fluffy cushion and a blanket."

"We'll never get him back now!" said Bart grumpily.

"Course we will!" exclaimed Toby. "Gargoylz to the rescue!" He bounced off the bed and made for the door.

"You can't go down," Ben told him. "You'll be seen."

Toby's face fell.

"Don't worry," said Max. "I've got a plan – secret plan: Gargoyle Chain. Agent Neal, the sitting-room window is right under yours, correct?"

Ben nodded. "Correct, Agent Black." "Then this is what we do," Max said. "You hold Barney's feet and dangle him out of the window, Barney holds Bart's feet,

Bart holds Toby's,
Toby holds Eli's and
Eli holds Zack's so that
Zack is at the bottom,
level with the sitting-
room window. A chain
of gargoylz!"

"Sounds dangerous,"
huffed Bart.

Ben grinned. "Will be
for me if Barney does a
bottom burp!"

"Sounds fun," said
Toby. "As good as a prank!"

Zack, Eli and Barney nodded in
agreement.

"Zack makes himself invisible so
Arabella doesn't see him," Max went on.
"Then he swings in through the window
and grabs Theo. Simple."

"And I haul them up to safety," finished
Ben. "Brilliant plan, Agent Black. But what
if Arabella sees Theo being whisked away?"

"She won't," said Max. "I'll go down
and cunningly distract her. When she finds

Theo's gone she'll just think he jumped
out of the window. It can't fail!" He strode
over to the door. "Wish me luck," he
said grimly. "I'm going into dangerous
territory."

Max peeped round the sitting-room door.
His radar went into overdrive: pigtails
bobbing, school badge gleaming, simpering
smile all over her face. He knew what that
meant. It was Enemy Agent Arabella Neal,

Codename:
Manic
monitor

Ben's sister, codename:
Manic Monitor.

"What are you
doing here?" said
Arabella suspiciously
when she saw him
creep in. "Keep away
from my new kitten."

"What a lovely
little tabby!" Max
managed to say, edging towards Theo,
who was curled up in his bed, purring.
"Where did you get it?"

"Poor Fluffikins was stuck up a tree,"
said Arabella. "He was so scared he was
stiff as a statue. Now he needs to recover.
So don't disturb him."

Max realized that Theo must have been
on his way to the sleepover when he'd
been surprised by a human – Arabella –
though it was hard to think of Ben's sister
as human. The little gargoyle had frozen

306

on the spot and Arabella had grabbed him.

Max took another step towards the window. He had to distract Arabella. The gargoyle chain must be ready by now.

"Cool!" he said suddenly, pointing towards the opposite corner of the room. "Look! There's a dear little mouse on the floor over there."

Arabella swung round to look. "A mouse!" she gasped. "I'd better pick it up before Fluffikins sees it."

She got down on her hands and knees and crawled into the corner.

Perfect! thought Max. He quickly undid the latch on the window and pushed it open wide.

"We've come to rescue you, Theo," he whispered.

To his surprise the kitten gave him a very cross glare. "Go away!" it mewed.

"I can't see a mouse." Arabella pouted as she stood up again. "Are you playing one of your silly tricks?"

Max rushed over to her side. "It was there, honest!" he exclaimed, pointing under a table. "I'm too clumsy to get it. You try. It probably won't be so scared of you."

Arabella dived under the table. Max glanced back at the window – just as Theo put out a determined paw and shut it!

As he did so there was a **thump** and Zack appeared, flattened against the pane of glass. He looked very surprised. The next minute he was whisked up out of sight and Max heard faint cackles of gargoyle laughter.

He zoomed out of the room, leaving Arabella under the table. He had to find his friends and work out a new plan.

When Max got back upstairs, Zack was sitting on the bed. His nose was bright red.

"Ssso much for the gargoyle chain," said Eli. "Although it was fun hanging upside down."

"Can we do it again?" asked Barney, the spikes on his back rippling hopefully.

"No!" declared Zack, rubbing his nose.

"I haven't laughed so much since we put pepper in the vicar's hymn book," said Toby.

"Trouble is," Max pointed out, "Theo's having a really good time. He doesn't want to be rescued!"

"He's been brainwashed by your sister,

Ben!" said Bart solemnly. "I think he's doomed."

"We don't seem to be cheering Bart up much," Max whispered to Ben. "He's gloomier than ever. And we can't start the sleepover without Theo."

"We'll soon change that," said Ben, "with my new plan." He dashed out of the room and was soon back carrying a furry toy cat. "Secret Plan: Swap the Cats. Agent Black, you distract Arabella. I'll grab Theo and put this toy cat in his place. It looks a bit like him."

"Stay here, gargoylz," said Max as they set off downstairs. "We'll soon have your friend back."

Ben put the toy cat behind his back and the two boys stepped boldly into the sitting room. Arabella was brushing Theo's coat. Theo seemed to be enjoying it. The boys stood there open-mouthed at the soppy scene.

"There wasn't a mouse," said Arabella
accusingly as soon as she saw them. "That
was a stupid trick, Max."

Max gulped. How was he going to
distract her this time? He'd have to talk
to her. And that meant girly chat! Yuck!
But he had to do it or Theo would be lost
for good.

"How could you think that dear little mouse was a trick?" he said, pretending to be hurt. "It was such a sweet little thing with its bright pink eyes and bright pink . . . ears and everything . . ."

Arabella sniffed crossly.

". . . and you could have made such a cute little home for it," Max ploughed on in a yucky voice. He could see that Arabella's eyes now had a faraway look as she thought about this. "You could have called it 'Squeaky's Palace' . . . or something sweet like that . . ." He glanced over at Ben, wondering how long he was going to have to keep up this ghastly rubbish.

Then he heaved a sigh of relief. Ben had made the switch and was already halfway out of the room with Theo in his arms. Max was just starting to follow when Theo let out a loud, indignant **Meow**!

"Fluffikins!" shrieked Arabella, startled out of her daydream. "How dare you! Give him back!" She snatched Theo from Ben. "I'm fed up with you two and your tricks," she snapped, throwing the toy cat at the boys. "Just go away and don't come back!"

Theo looked extremely smug as Arabella settled him back down in his bed and launched into a soothing lullaby.

"I can't believe it," said Ben, throwing the

toy cat onto the bed. "Theo doesn't even mind Arabella's dreadful singing. She'll be dressing him up next!"

"Spluttering gutterz!" declared Toby, flapping his wings in excitement. "That's given me an idea for the next plan. Find something really terrible that Theo would hate to wear, then tell your sister he'd love it. That should do the trick! Theo will be out of there before you can say whooshing waterspouts."

 Ben looked at the toy cat. It was wearing a pink collar with sparkling diamond studs. "What about this!" he exclaimed, pulling it off and waving it in the air. "Secret Plan: Pink Horror."

"Just the thing!" chorused the gargoylz.

"Don't be surprised if he likes it," muttered Bart.

"Not you two again!" tutted Arabella in disgust as Ben and Max sidled into the sitting room once more.

"We've just come to say sorry," said Max. "Haven't we, Ben?"

Ben nodded. "And to give you something nice for your new kitten to wear." He held out the collar.

Arabella snatched it and inspected it suspiciously.

"No tricks," said Max solemnly. "It's just a nice sparkly collar – it'll look much better on your kitten than on that silly stuffed toy."

"It *is* very sweet," cooed Arabella, advancing on Theo, who was curled up in his rug, eyes closed. "Look what I've got here, Fluffikins." She dangled the collar in front of him.

Max and Ben held their breath.
At the sound of Arabella's voice
Theo woke up. Then he
saw the collar in her
hands. It sparkled
in the sunlight.
He leaped out of
his bed with a
horrified yowl
and raced around
the room.
Arabella chased
after him. "Come
back!" she shrieked,
knocking over vases and
scattering newspapers.
Max and Ben burst out
laughing – then stopped
abruptly as the sitting-room

door was flung open and
Ben's mum rushed in. Max
looked at Ben in horror.
How would they
ever rescue Theo now?

"What's going
on, Arabella?" she
demanded. "And
what is that kitten
doing here?"

"I found it up
next door's tree,"
panted Arabella,
making a dive for
Theo's tail. "I'm
looking after it."

"Take it back straight
away," said her mother.

"It's not yours and the neighbours will be missing it."

"But, Mum—" wailed Arabella.

"No arguments," said Mum firmly.

"Why don't Max and I take the kitten back?" suggested Ben. "We don't mind," he added, opening his blue eyes wide and looking helpful.

"That would be very kind." Mum smiled gratefully at the boys.

"You won't be able to catch him," said Arabella nastily.

Ben walked towards the kitten. Theo gave a meow and leaped into his arms. Ben smiled innocently and he and Max sped out of the door, leaving Arabella fuming.

The boys burst into the bedroom to a rousing cheer from the gargoylz, who gathered

around Theo as he wriggled back into his gargoyle shape.

"Thank you for rescuing me," he said. "I enjoyed being fussed over, but that collar was too much. If that's what kittens have to wear I'll never let myself get caught again!"

"Now that's all sorted out," said Ben, "we can get on with having fun."

Bart's ears pricked up. "Fun?" he said. "What sort of fun?"

Max winked at Ben. Bart was cheering up at last.

Max grinned. "Just you wait and see. This sleepover's going to be awesome."

4. Midnight Feast Fun

Max looked at his gargoyle friends, who were sitting in a row on Ben's bed, and grinned. "This is going to be the best sleepover ever!" he declared. "What shall we do first?"

"Cookiez and cake! Cookiez and cake!" shouted Zack, jumping up and down on the duvet.

"They're for later," Max told him. "Ben and I have only just had supper. Anyway, we have to eat them at midnight. That's why it's called a midnight feast."

"Let's play a game," suggested Ben.

"Good thinking, Agent Neal," said Max. "How about Twister?"

The gargoylz looked puzzled. Max got out a box and laid a big plastic sheet over the floor. On the sheet were different coloured circles.

Toby, Barney and Zack immediately leaped off the bed and jumped in and out of the circles.

Eli turned into a snake and slithered around, tripping them all up.

"Everyone off," laughed Ben. "The game hasn't started yet."

The gargoylz reluctantly stepped off the mat.

"Each time I call out a colour you all put one paw on a circle of that colour," explained Max. He spun an arrow on a card. "And this will tell you which paw. Look, put your front left paw on a red circle and keep it there." He spun again. "Now left back on a green circle. Last one to fall over wins. Eli, you need your paws so you'd better change back."

"Come and join in, Bart," said Ben. "It's a lot of fun."

"Certainly not," grumbled Bart. "Looks much too dangerous to me." And he hid his face in his gladiator skirt.

"Come on, Bart," said Zack, patting him on the back and knocking him off the bed.

"Just one game then," mumbled Bart.

Soon the mat was a tangle of scrambling gargoylz, with Bart in the middle, a big grin on his face.

"I'm winning!" Bart declared.

"That's because you're sitting on my wing," moaned Toby.

Suddenly they heard footsteps outside. The gargoylz dived under a chest of drawers just as Ben's mum stuck her head round the door.

"It's getting late, boys," she said, smiling. "No more jumping about. Time to settle down."

She went out again, closing the door. The gargoylz crawled out as Max and Ben quickly pulled on their pyjamas.

"Good game!" exclaimed Zack.

Bart nodded. "Very enjoyable. Especially as I won!"

"No you didn't," laughed Barney. "You pushed us all over!"

"Didn't!" said Bart.

"Did!" said all the other gargoylz.

"Shhhh!" warned Ben. "Mum'll hear."
He pulled out a lilo and began to blow it
up with a foot pump.

"What's that?" asked Theo, poking the
flabby plastic with his paw.

"It's Max's bed," said Ben.

The gargoylz immediately jumped
onto the lilo and rolled about as it
filled with air.

"There's only one thing wrong with this sssleepover," said Eli. "Ben's got his bed and Max has got the ssspare one. Where are *we* going to sssleep?"

"I hadn't thought of that," said Ben. "How about hanging off the windowsill? Or would you feel more at home dangling from the bookshelves?"

"But it's not a proper sssleepover if we don't have a bed like you," said Eli.

Ben ran to the cupboard. "I've got an idea," he grunted as he pulled a sleeping bag and a couple of pillows off the top shelf. "You can sleep in this. It should be big enough for you all."

He opened the sleeping bag up and folded it so that it looked like a bed, with the pillows arranged at the top. The gargoylz piled in excitedly.

"Move up, Zack," said Toby. "And stop those snakes wriggling about, Eli. They tickle. That's it – now we all fit."

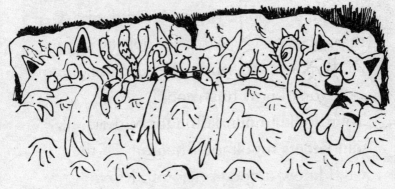

Ben put his bedside light on and turned the main one off.

"This is so cosy," purred Theo. "Much better than that bed your sister made."

"Lovely," yawned Barney. "So comfortable . . ." His voice faded out and he fell asleep.

Toby nudged him. "You've got to stay awake for the midnight feast."

Barney jerked awake. "Sorry," he said, with his eyes half closed.

"We've got to do something to keep

him awake," Ben told Max. "It's ages till midnight."

"I've got a plan!" Max winked at him. "Let's tell a spooky story. No one can sleep through that."

"Brilliant, Agent Black," said Ben.

"Don't know any spooky stories," said Toby, looking puzzled. "Do we, gargoylz?" The others shook their heads.

"I know a good one," said Max. "Turn your light off, Ben. We need my multicoloured torch for this."

He sat down next to Ben. Then he shone his torch up under his chin, bathing his face in a ghostly green glow as he began his tale.

"Deep in the dark, dark wood lived a boy," he began in a creepy voice. "And

one dark, dark night he went out into the
dark, dark wood and—"

He stopped. There were footsteps on the
landing outside, getting nearer.

"Dangling drainpipes!" squeaked
Barney, his floppy ears pricked up with
fright. "It's something scary coming to
get us!"

"Worse than that," said Ben. "It's my
parents. They must be on their way to bed.
Quiet, everybody."

Max turned off his torch and they all
sat in the dark, listening as the footsteps
went past the door. The footsteps continued

into Ben's parents' bedroom and the door
closed. Max switched on the torch again.

"Where was I?" He grinned horribly in the torchlight.

"The dark, dark wood," said Theo in a tiny voice.

"Oh yes. The boy went out into the dark, dark wood and what did he see?"

The gargoylz' eyes grew wider and wider.

"A monster?" whispered Barney.

"A zombie?" quavered Eli, his snakes trembling.

"No," said Max. "He saw something white . . . and floaty . . . and it was coming towards him . . ."

"A ghost!" shrieked the gargoylz in terror.

"It was his friend under a sheet," Max laughed. "He'd dressed up to scare him!"

He shone his torch around the room. The gargoylz were lying in a trembling row, eyes like saucers, clutching the sleeping bag.

"All awake, I see," said Ben cheerfully.

"Wouldn't dare go to sleep after that story," whimpered Bart. "It was too scary."

Toby crawled up onto Ben's bed and gave Max a nudge. "I don't think scary stories are a good idea," he whispered. "Not if we want to cheer Bart up."

"You're right," said Max.

"How about telling jokes?" suggested Ben.

"Jokessssss?" Eli looked puzzled. He turned to Theo. "What are jokessss?"

"I don't know," Theo said with a shrug and the other gargoylz shook their heads.

"Jokes are very short, very funny stories," explained Max. "They're meant to make you laugh. Listen – why was the sand wet?"

"We don't know," said Zack. "Why *was* the sand wet?"

Max grinned. "Because the sea weed!"

"Seaweed?" The gargoylz looked at each other in bafflement.

Then Toby burst out laughing. "The sea did a wee! That's what made the sand wet!" he explained to his friends. Soon they were all rolling around on the floor holding their sides. Even Bart stopped looking scared and managed a grin.

"We've got loads more where that came from," said Ben. "What flies through the air and wobbles?"

"I don't know," chorused the gargoylz, their eyes shining in the torchlight.

"A jelly-copter!" giggled Ben.

"My turn," said Max. "Why didn't the skeleton go to the party? Because he had no*body* to go with!"

The gargoylz shook with laughter in their little bed. Then they all heard a strange noise. It was a wheezy, slurpy sound like water draining down a rusty old plughole. They looked in amazement to see Bart holding onto his sides and rocking backwards and forwards.

"Now I understand jokes," he spluttered. "Listen, I've got one. What do you call a pipe that rain runs along?"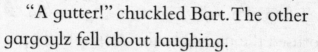

"I don't know," said Ben. "What *do* you call a pipe that rain runs along?"

"A gutter!" chuckled Bart. The other gargoylz fell about laughing.

"That was the best one yet," wheezed Toby, tears of laughter running down his stony cheeks.

"Gutter!" repeated Zack, holding his sides.

Max looked at Ben. "Why is that funny?" he whispered.

"Beats me," said Ben. "I don't think Bart's quite got the hang of jokes yet."

"Well, at least it's cheered him up," Max said happily.

"Gutter!" Bart guffawed loudly, slapping his skirts.

"We'll have to keep the noise down," warned Ben. "My parents might hear – or worse, we might wake up my sister!"

The gargoylz all stopped laughing and looked horrified at the thought.

"Not Arabella!" Theo growled.

Max listened at the door. "It's OK," he said after a moment. "I think everyone's asleep. Time for the midnight feast!"

The gargoylz jumped up and down in excitement as Ben pulled out the bottle of fizzy drink and the chocolate cake.

"Cookiez first! Cookiez first!" chanted Zack, diving under the bed for the box.

Max took off the lid and

his face fell. "I might have known!" he exclaimed bitterly. "Look what my stupid sister's done with the icing."

The others peered into the box. All the cookies were bright girly pink – and decorated with sparkly icing stars and fairies. Some of them had writing on.

Max picked up the biggest cookie. "*Boys smell*," he read.

"Here's another one," said Toby. "*Boys are stupid*."

The gargoylz hooted with laughter.

"What do you call a boy with girly cookiez?" chortled Bart.

"I don't know," said Toby, his eyes bright with mischief.

"MAX!" crowed Bart.

The gargoylz rolled about their bed in delight.

Max took the cookie box and sat on his bed. "Well, if only girls eat pink cookies, then you lot won't be wanting any

and I've got them all to myself," he said
smugly, taking a big bite. "Delicious!" he
sighed.

"We didn't say we didn't want one," said
Barney, horrified. "I'm sure they're lovely."

"Yes." Toby nodded hurriedly. "Pink
cookiez are probably the best. We'd better
taste one to make sure."

Max grinned. "Go on then. Pass the
choccy cake, Ben."

For the next ten minutes the only
sound that could be heard was a happy
chomping and slurping. Bart made them
all giggle when the fizzy drink made him
burp and spiders came tumbling out of his
mouth.

Soon there were only a few cookies left.

"Dangling drainpipes!" said Toby, leaning back, his hands over his fat belly. "That was lovely."

"What do we do next on a sleepover?" asked Theo.

"Well, we could go to sleep, I suppose," said Ben.

"More jokes!" came Bart's gurgly voice.

"OK," said Ben. "Why did the ghost—"

"Quiet!" said Toby. "There are footsteps approaching."

"I can't hear anything," whispered Max, listening hard.

"Gargoylz have sssuper-sssensitive hearing," said Eli. "I can hear them too."

"Hide!" hissed Ben as he dived beneath his covers. Max jumped onto his bed. He heard the gargoylz scuttle under Ben's bed, dragging the cake tins with them. He suddenly remembered the drink. He grabbed the bottle, shoved it under his duvet and switched off the torch. And just in time.

The door to the bedroom was flung open and a figure stood there, outlined by the landing light. Max's radar burst into life: fluffy slippers, frilly nightdress, a look that could kill at ten paces. He knew what that meant. It was Enemy Agent Arabella Neal. Codename: Manic Monitor.

"Got you!" shouted Arabella. "You're mucking around and I'm telling. You're in big trouble and you deserve it after taking away my kitten. MUM! DAD!"

Footsteps could be heard running along the landing. Max knew he had to do something quickly. He had an idea. "What's going on?" he groaned as Ben's dad came into the room. Then he sat up and rubbed his eyes. "Why did you wake me up?"

Ben pretended he was still asleep. "I'm having a nightmare!" he wailed. "There's a monster in the doorway. It's got fluffy slippers and it's *sooo* ugly."

"Arabella!" Ben's dad sounded angry. "What are you doing out of bed?"

"The boys were—"

"Is this your idea of a joke?" growled Ben's dad. "The boys were fast asleep and you've woken them up. Go to bed – and I don't want to hear another peep out of you until morning."

Arabella stomped off.

"Sorry, boys," whispered
Ben's dad. "Back to sleep now."
He closed the door softly.

When it was safe,
Max switched
on the torch.

"There are still
some cookies left," Ben
said, peering into the tin. The
gargoylz scrambled eagerly
out from under the bed and
tucked in.

"I haven't had such a tasty feast
since I ate the vicar's holly bush," said Toby
happily, wiping crumbs from his mouth.

"I've got another joke," declared Bart.
"What did the cookie say when his friend
was run over by a steamroller?"

"Tell us, Bart," said Max, exchanging
a look with Ben. He could tell they were
both wondering if it would be a real joke
this time or another 'Bart Special'.

"He said, 'Oh, crumbs!'" said Bart proudly, a huge grin spreading over his face.

Max and Ben did a high-five as their gargoyle friends bounced around and laughed uproariously.

"Success, Agent Black," said Ben. "Not only have we outwitted Arabella and cheered up Bart, but he's got the hang of jokes!"

"Missions accomplished, Agent Neal," agreed Max. "This is officially the best sleepover in the history of sleepovers!"

Gargoylz Fact File

Full name: Tobias the Third
Known as: Toby
Special Power: Flying
Likes: All kinds of pranks and mischief
– especially playing jokes on the vicar
Dislikes: Mrs Hogsbottom, garden gnomes

Full name: Barnabas
Known as: Barney
Special Power: Making big stinks!
Likes: Cookiez
Dislikes: Being surprised by humanz

Full name: Eli
Special Power: Turning into
a grass snake
Likes: Sssports Day, ssslithering
Dislikes: Ssscary ssstories

Full name: Bartholomew

Known as: Bart

Special Power: Burping spiders

Likes: Being grumpy

Dislikes: Being told to cheer up

Full name: Theophilus

Known as: Theo

Special Power: Turning into a ferocious tiger (well, tabby kitten!)

Likes: Sunny spots and cosy places

Dislikes: Rain

Full name: Zackary

Known as: Zack

Special Power: Making himself invisible to humanz

Likes: Bouncing around, eating bramblz, thistlz, and anything with Pricklz!

Dislikes: Keeping still

Full name: Ira
SPECIAL POWER: Making it rain
Likes: Making humans walk the plank

Dislikes: Being bored

Name: Azzan
SPECIAL POWER: Breathing fir

Likes: Surprises

Dislikes: Smoke going up
his nose and making him sneeze

Gargoylz Take a Trip

Burchett and Vogler

Max and Ben are looking forward to
fun, sea and sand on a school trip to
the beach. But the Gargoylz are
deteremined to go too, which means
more tricks, more pranks and double
trouble – now the boys can't wait!

Don't miss the fun! Join in with the four
new Gargoylz adventures in this book!

RED FOX

978 1 862 30867 1

Gargoylz Put on a Show

Burchett and Vogler

Max and Ben are in the school play,
and the Gargoylz are very excited. But
will Ben remember his lines? Will the
wolf costume be fierce enough? And
what happens when the Gargoylz decide
they want starring roles too?

The Show must go on! Join Max,
Ben and the Gargoylz in four fun new
adventures inside this book!

RED FOX

978 1 849 41033 5

Coming soon!

Gargoylz Have Fun at the Fair

Burchett and Vogler

The fair has come to town and Max, Ben and the Gargoylz can't wait to ride the ghost train, zoom along on the dodgems and zip down the helter-skelter. But Barney gets trapped! Can the boys save their friend and outwit Ben's evil older sister, Enemy Agent Arabella, too?

Find out in the four exciting adventures inside this book!

RED FOX

978 1 849 41034 2